Point the Finger of Blame

DEREK SMITH

Text copyright © Derek Smith 2014
Design copyright © Max Cartwright 2014
All rights reserved.

Derek Smith has asserted his right under the Copyright, Designs and Patents Act 1988 to be identified as the author of this work.

This book is a work of fiction. Names and characters are the product of the author's imagination and any resemblance to actual persons, living or dead, is entirely coincidental.

No part of this book may be reprinted or reproduced or utilised in any form or by electronic, mechanical or any other means, now known or hereafter invented, including photocopying or recording, or in any information storage or retrieval system, without the permission in writing from the Publisher and Author.

First published 2014
By Rowanvale Books
57, Brynllwchwr Road,
Loughor,
Swansea
SA4 6SQ
www.rowanvalebooks.com

A CIP catalogue record for this book is available from the British Library.
ISBN: 978-1-909902-43-5

Point the Finger of Blame

DEREK SMITH

PROLOGUE

In the beautiful countryside, on the side of a hill, sat a man in his late sixties; he was looking out across the land which he had worked on and known all of his life. He was the estate's gamekeeper, or gillie, and this had been his favourite spot for as long as he could remember. Sat there alone he, for the first time in his life, allowed the tears to fall without check. No one should lose their child; it wasn't natural. They'd only had the one boy. Now he was gone and nothing could change that; all the words he wished he had said would now never be spoken. He'd hoped that his son would follow in his footsteps. It wasn't to be. He remembered how happy he had been when he met and married his wife; their lives had been made complete with the birth of their son.

His son Jimmy had shared his love of the country and its creatures, and loved to learn about all aspects of life. The family had come though the Second World War and his son had come home safely after serving in the Korean War. It had changed all their lives once it was over. He couldn't help but wish he could turn back the clock and do things differently.

He looked back on his son's childhood with fondness, trying to remember those happy times and forget the later sadness. He sat until the sun went down, and then took the familiar path back to his home, where he knew he would find his wife waiting for him: tears in her eyes and pain in her heart.

CHAPTER ONE

Brian sat looking across the valley; his gun was carefully balanced across his knees and he had a thoughtful expression on his weather-beaten face. He had two dogs resting at his feet. Seeing something move to the right, he turned his head slowly to see a herd of red deer, just coming into view. They looked wonderful; the mountains and the loch loomed in the background. The dogs had taken no notice of the deer - they were too well trained for that. Brian had lived here all his life but never tired of this spot. All the land he could see was part of the Ghias Estate. The estate was situated North-West of the border of England; it was the property of the Laird and Lady MacCulloch, who had inherited it on the death of the Laird's father. The estate covered 4,000 acres and two rivers ran through the land, one of which connected the two lochs. The small loch was visible to Brian but the larger one, being about a mile and a half long and four hundred yards wide, was further down the valley. Some of the flatter land was used to grow crops, and several hundred acres were kept as forest and harvested for wood. Although sheep grazed the lower slopes and the prize herd of Aberdeen

Angus were kept in the fields closer to the estate farm, it was the wild places where most of the red deer were found and the golden eagle flew. It was these steep and wild places that Brian loved the best and, as he was the estate's gillie (or gamekeeper as the Laird preferred to call him) they came under his control, although mainly suitable for hunting and shooting.

Brian had been raised on the estate. When his father, the previous gillie, had passed on, the Laird had given the job to Brian. From a small boy, Brian had learnt the many crafts needed to keep the estate in good order for the shoots that took place. As well as this, he was responsible for keeping the rivers in a good condition for fishing. The red deer that Brian had been watching would be stalked by the frequent visitors to the estate.

Standing up, Brian picked up a bag full of rabbits and wood pigeons (which he had shot earlier), turned and walked, following the track that had been made by the red deer over the years. His dogs walked faithfully behind him, needing no instruction along the familiar path. Eventually, he spotted a group of small houses at the base of the mountain, sheltered from the cold winds that blew in the long winter months. Off to one side, and a short distance away from the others, stood the far grander house: the Laird's residence. In his mind, Brian had always thought of it as a mansion - too large for one family. But, it wasn't for him to question such things.

The gamekeeper's house was larger than most of the cottages on the estate, so he kept his thoughts to himself. Brian had never been one for rocking the status quo; he was, on the whole, content with his lot; he never saw himself working anywhere but on the estate. To one side of the Laird's house ran the second of the two rivers, and on its far bank stood the water wheel that generated the electricity for the house. Further down the river, just around the bend, was a second water wheel that pumped water for the estate. All the estate workers were supplied with running water and all felt fortunate. He knew that on some of the neighbouring estates, the owners were not so generous and many workers still had to collect their water every day. All in all, the estate workers were well treated and felt themselves fortunate to work for the present Laird and Lady MacCulloch. Yet, Brian still missed the previous Laird who had passed on a couple of years before. The present Laird's father had gone right though the Great Depression, only to fall from his horse and break his neck just as things were improving. Though, at the same time, he was glad for the present Laird; times were changing and a fresh mind was needed.

As Brian got closer to the main house, he turned toward the servants' entrance. After wiping his feet, he opened the door and entered the kitchen. His dogs settled down on a patch of grass near the door and waited. It was part of Brian's duties to keep the house stocked with game, and the rabbits and pigeons would be well received for staff meals. The better quality meats like grouse, venison and pheasant were for the Laird and Lady. Brian always looked forward to his cup of tea so that he could catch up with the latest news from the house. Today, however, no one seemed to notice him as he entered. There was a new face in the kitchen. One he hadn't seen before. After giving a small cough to attract Cook's attention, he was soon being introduced to the centre of attention.

'I've got a new helper at last!' exclaimed Agnes, the Laird's cook.

She had worked for the estate as long as he could remember and had worked her way up to her present position. She was a large woman who clearly loved the food she cooked and Brian had never seen her without a smile on her face in all the years that he had known her; she seemed able to find a positive outlook on everything. As she was called Cook by everyone, he seldom heard her being called by her given name.

'This is June Duff. The mistress said I could have help; the estate is doing well this year and with all the extra visitors expected I will certainly need it.'

Brian always felt uncomfortable in the presence of young lasses whom he hadn't met before. But he liked what he saw. Although not especially pretty, she had a good figure and a lovely smile. Before he had time to say anything, Cook started to speak again.

'June has come from Oban to work here as a kitchen maid. It's her first job and she's lucky to get it, what with so many still being out of work.' Stopping to pause for breath, she turned to June who was looking at Brian with interest.

He wasn't a tall man, standing at about five foot nine, and he was stocky in build. But June thought he had a nice face, although very weather beaten and wild looking, with a mass of red hair.

'This is Brian. He's the estate gamekeeper. Look what he's brought us.'

With that, June looked down at Brian's contribution to the day's menu.

Point the Finger of Blame

'Don't just look at them girl, take them and hang them in the meat store while I give the good man his drink of tea!'

With that, June rushed forward and took the rabbits into the side room to be cleaned.

So, this was their first brief meeting. Neither of them realised how soon they would become good friends. At thirty years old, he was a good ten years older than June, but over the next few weeks they found that they seemed to have a lot in common. Brian found himself looking forward to his visits to the kitchen - and not just for his cup of tea. Brian offered to show June some of the countryside near the house. Their friendship was slowly developing into something deeper. Unfortunately, they realised that this would be frowned upon as staff were not expected to fraternize with each other. The old Laird had been concerned that it might cause the estate to lose a worker and not many wanted to work in such a remote spot.

Once the pair realised their feelings for each other were growing deeper, they began to meet secretly. June would tell Cook she was going for a walk to get some exercise in her free time. Suspecting nothing, Cook approved; she was a great believer in the health benefits of fresh air and so encouraged her young helper. Then, June would walk down to the river and meet Brian, who would sometimes take the duck punt out amid the reeds so to be out of sight of prying eyes. Sometimes, they would follow the river away from the house into the mountain valleys. The couple would spend as much time together as they could. They talked about everything; June wanted to know all about the animals and birds that they saw. Time always passed quickly for the couple.

To June, Brian seemed a mild mannered and kind man who was fanatical about his work. Yet sometimes, a harder side to his nature showed itself to June. Once, spotting a fox in the distance, June was surprised at his attitude towards the beautiful animal. To Brian, the fox was vermin, something that needed to be trapped or shot.

Seeing her puzzled expression, Brian explained: 'June, I know they look pretty to you, but I wouldn't be doing my job if I didn't keep their numbers down. They kill the pheasants and other game birds; the estate relies on the shooting. It's no different than shooting the rabbits you have for the kitchen. These vermin need keeping under control or they would take over.'

June realised by the tone of his voice that nothing would alter his view. But, to her, the fox was a beautiful animal and she couldn't see what real harm it could do. Over the next few months, June learnt a great deal about the countryside and its inhabitants. It wasn't long before she could recognise most of the birds by sight as well as song. Brian taught her the names of the wild flowers growing in the area and was soon as besotted with the wild places as Brian was. Brought up in Oban, she had never had the freedom to roam around the surrounding countryside. Instead, she played in the streets with her friends. Her parents had always been too busy trying to make a living to be able to take her out to the countryside; even if they had, they wouldn't have been able to teach her much as they too were brought up in the town.

Point the Finger of Blame

June knew that Brian had two gun dogs, a red setter and a spaniel, but they had never taken them out on the walks. So, one Sunday, she asked Brian if they could take them along as she would like to get to know them. Brian turned quite frosty:

'They are working dogs. I don't let anyone get friendly with 'um. They are one-man dogs and that's how it's going to stay. They're the best gun dogs in the area; working with anyone else would ruin them.'

June was surprised at the tone of his voice and couldn't stop the tear at the corner of her eye. When Brian saw that he had upset her, he put his hands on her shoulders and, looking into her face, he said:

'They are working dogs June. They love what they do and they're good at what they do. They aren't pets and they can't be treated as such. If you started to treat them like pets, they would be ruined for work.'

June gave Brian a small smile. 'Alright, I won't ask again.'

June didn't really understand, but she knew from Brian's tone of voice there was no point in continuing with the idea.

'Come on June, I'll take you fishing.'

June wasn't sure she would like that, but she agreed and they went off to the river. Brian had clearly planned this as his fishing kit was hidden behind a mound at the river's bend. June soon got bored sitting on the bank and started messing about. At first, Brian continued to concentrate on the fishing: he soon got distracted. He started to chase her playfully around a clump of trees at the water's edge. It wasn't long before he caught her and, with his arms around her waist, they fell to the ground. June turned onto her back, giggling as she looked into his eyes. Leaning up on one elbow, Brian met her gaze. June's giggling stopped. Their lips met and they kissed for the first time. At that moment, her mother's words about waiting until she was married came into June's mind. She gently pushed Brian away.

'I think we had better get back to the fishing.'

Brian smiled at her. He understood why she had pushed him away and thought it was just as well; he wasn't sure how far he would have gone.

'I think we had better pack up and get you back to the house.'

They both knew that, from that moment, something had changed in their relationship: they were meant for each other. They walked back to the house in silence: both happy. Just before they got in sight of the big house, Brian turned off towards his cottage and June went back to the kitchens. Both had smiles on their faces.

They continued to see each other whenever they had the chance. But things came to a head one day when they were watching some swans on the lake.

'Did you know that swans mate for life?' Brian asked. Without waiting for a reply, he went on. 'That's how it should be, make sure you've got the right one and then stay together.'

He took hold of one of June's hands and looked straight into her eyes. 'Will you marry me June?'

June looked at Brian, unsure at first if she had heard him correctly. Brian thought she was thinking of a reason to say no and his face started to fall. He had thought they were getting on so well; had he misread the situation?

Point the Finger of Blame

Seeing his expression she laughed. 'Did you just ask me to marry you?'

Brian nodded, unable to speak.

'Of course I will, I thought you'd never ask!'

It was Brian's turn to pause. Then he grabbed June and kissed her.

June was overjoyed at the prospect of marrying Brian. She insisted that he would have to ask her father's permission first. The Laird's permission would also have to be sought, as was the custom, though Brian wasn't sure how the Laird would react. For the first time, Brian was happy that there was a new Laird and hoped that he would be more open minded than the previous Laird would have been. The couple were very happy, but decided to keep their secret until the Laird and June's father had agreed.

With some trepidation, Brian smartened himself up a few days later to see the Laird, who was surprised when the butler said that Brian wished to speak with him. Normally, their meetings were instigated by the Laird and not Brian. The butler took Brian out to the walled garden where the Laird was sitting under an apple tree. A good looking man in his early forties, he was fit and athletic in build, and had been in charge of the estate for nearly three years now. After a hesitant start, Brian found him easier to deal with than the previous Laird, who, although Brian had had great respect and affection for him, had been a very stern man. Much to Brian's surprise he found himself a bag of nerves.

'Hello Brian. I hope nothing's wrong; it's not like you to ask for a meeting.'

Brian took a deep breath. Seeing the gamekeeper's nervousness, the Laird offered him a seat.

'What is it you wanted to see me about? You're not leaving are you? That pest of a neighbour hasn't been trying to poach you off of me again has he?'

'No Sir, I don't intend to leave.'

Taking a deep breath and squaring his shoulders, Brian plucked up the courage to speak.

'I have come to ask your permission to marry June Duff.' Not stopping in fear that he was to be refused, Brian continued, 'I know you don't like staff fraternising but we want to spend the rest of our days together...'

The Laird held up his hand before Brian could say anymore.

'Does this mean that I am going to need to find new help in the kitchen so soon?'

'No Sir!' exclaimed Brian, 'There's no reason for that, Sir. I would be happy for June to keep her job in the kitchens.'

With that, Lady MacCulloch stepped out from behind the shrubbery.

'I heard what you asked, Brian, and you must know that we wouldn't have stopped you two marrying. Would we, darling?'

She turned and smiled sweetly at her husband. The Laird began to stutter in frustration but, realising that it was no good to argue with his wife, he turned back to Brian.

'I was going to make you fret a bit but, as my wife has pointed out, I wouldn't dream of not giving you our blessing. You're a good man and she's a lucky lass. I don't follow everything my father did and I realise that you can't have men and women together without this sort of thing happening. When are you thinking of getting married?'

Brian was so taken aback by the reaction that he took a few minutes before replying.

'I need to go and ask June's father for permission first, Sir.'

'Of course, one must do things properly. Well, you can both have the day off tomorrow and go to ask June's father for his blessing.'

Brian was pleased and a little bit surprised at how easily it had all gone. Thanking the Laird and Lady MacCulloch, he turned and walked back to the kitchen to tell June.

As he entered the kitchen, he could tell that June had told Cook her news. They both stared at him, awaiting the result of his visit to the big house. Brian tried to look disappointed but it didn't fool June; she screamed her delight and threw herself into his arms. After telling them both what had happened, he turned to June:

'The Laird has given us both the day off tomorrow to go and speak to your father. Let's hope he agrees just as easily.'

June looked thoughtful, 'I don't see why not. After all, you're a good catch.' She grinned as she looked at him. 'He'll probably be pleased to have me married off.'

Secretly, she wasn't so sure and she crossed her fingers behind her back. She knew her father could be difficult and, if he decided that the age difference was too large or he took a dislike to Brian for any reason, he could easily refuse.

'Well I never!' exclaimed Cook, 'I will make you a cake to take. That might soften him up.'

DEREK SMITH

The couple thanked Cook and then went back to their separate duties.

Both Brian and June spent a fretful night worrying about how things would go in the morning.

The next morning started well. The sun was shining and there was a pleasant breeze. Brian collected June and they set off on the ten mile walk to her family home in Oban. Neither of them spoke much; each was buried in their own thoughts. As they approached, Brian looked around with interest. He had never lived in a town, but he decided there and then that he wouldn't want to. To his mind the air was thick with smoke and, by the time they reached June's home, he couldn't see his beloved countryside. The house was in a terrace and was clearly very small compared to his home. It was a one up two down property. Going down the communal path that led to the back door, Brian saw there was an outhouse - part of which seemed to contain the shared toilet for the terrace. At the far end a woman was in the shared wash house. A tin bath hung on a nail outside.

June walked toward the house at the far end and shouted as she opened the back door.

'Hello Mum.'

From inside the house a woman's voice replied: 'Come in dear. This is a nice surprise! I wasn't expecting you to have a day off again so soon. Nothing wrong I hope?'

June's mother was stood by the stove, turning as they entered. Brian looked with interest at June's mother. She was a pleasant looking lady, with a pleasant smile and kindly eyes. Like so many of the women from the working classes, she was obviously used to hard work but strove to keep her house clean and tidy, despite the hard times. Brian turned at a slight noise and noticed a rugged looking man sitting next to the empty fireplace. The man obviously worked outside as his face was well tanned from the sun and he had a muscular frame. June quickly introduced Brian to her parents. June's father looked Brian up and down in a judgemental manner. June's mother said a brief hello and then turned back to the stove, continuing with her work. June's father looked at his daughter and asked:

'To what do we owe this honour young lady? It's not your day off; you haven't got the sack have you?'

Although his tone showed some concern, there was an undertone of worry in his voice. Times were hard and he couldn't afford another mouth to feed. Seeing his daughter's indignant expression, he realised his worries were unfounded, then, turned his attention to Brian:

'It's not often that June brings strangers back to the home. I hope you bin looking after her.'

Turning back to his daughter, without waiting for a reply, he continued: 'It's lucky you found us home, or unlucky depending on how you look at it; I've lost my job on the roads. If you as much as straighten your back nowadays, they fire you. It's damn hard to find more work.' He looked again at his daughter's face, his expression serious. 'Make sure you work hard or you'll be next.'

June looked at her father and at her mother who stood by the stove.

'Sorry to hear that, Dad. I haven't lost my job. I came home because Brian wants to ask you something.'

She turned to Brian with a look of encouragement. With that, Brian felt it best to waste no time. He introduced himself and told June's father of his intentions to wed her, before asking for his approval. June's father looked once more at Brian.

'You're a good bit older than June. Do you work at the estate?'

'I'm the gamekeeper,' Brian replied with pride in his voice. 'I can look after your daughter. I have a nice cottage that comes with the post, so she will have a good home.'

Brian was relieved to see that that seemed to impress June's father, so he went on to explain that June would be able to carry on working. That way, they might be able to help out a bit until the family's fortunes changed.

Both of June's parents looked relieved that their daughter would be taken care of, and June's father gladly gave his blessing.

'You mind you look after her; she's always been a good daughter and never caused us any worry. Since she hasn't introduced us properly, I'd better. I'm Jimmy and this is my wife Mary. You're too old to call us Mum and Dad.'

The couple both looked happy at the news and June's father turned once again to his daughter.

'I don't want to be a granddad yet mind, I'm not old enough!'

With that his wife gave him a friendly tap. 'Don't start already. Anyway, you're plenty old enough so don't kid yourself.'

Turning to the couple and giving them a large grin, she said in a kindly voice, 'Come on, let's have a cuppa and a chat. I want to know more about you, young man.'

With that, June got a parcel from her basket. After fetching a plate from the dresser, she returned with a fruit cake.

'Cook gave this to me so we could celebrate in style.'

With that, they all tucked in. June's parents were pleased for their daughter, and Jimmy's reservations about Brian's age were soon forgotten, as he realised that Brian could give his daughter a better life. After spending about an hour talking and getting to know one another, the couple said goodbye and set off back to the estate, promising to visit again as soon as they could.

CHAPTER TWO

It was three months later, on the 3rd June 1931, that the couple took their vows in a small chapel in Oban. It was a simple affair but the couple didn't care; they just wanted to be together as man and wife. June was thrilled that her parents had managed to attend. The couple were very happy as Brian slipped his mother's wedding ring onto June's finger. They soon settled into Brian's cottage and June made the place more homely, adding the touches that only a woman would think of. Although Brian had lived in the cottage all his life, he hadn't done much to it since his parents' death several years before. Because of this, June was able to make changes that didn't upset Brian. She loved having a place to call her own; it was bigger than she had ever been used to. Brian teased her about all the wild flowers that June had about the place.

'They'll live longer if you leave 'um where they grow!' he would say to her. She ignored his teasing.

The couple couldn't have been happier. They still went for walks whenever they had the chance but now it didn't matter who saw them. It wasn't long before June found out that she was pregnant. Their happiness was complete.

Their son was born on the 23rd April the following year. He was a bonny baby of 7lb 4oz and born with a mop of ginger hair. The couple were overjoyed with the new edition to the family; they chose to call him Jimmy, after June's father. Despite his previous comments, June's father was proud to be a grandfather and was obviously very proud that his grandson was to carry his name. They saw as much as they could of Jimmy junior. The couple doted on their son. Brian was sure that his son would be the next gamekeeper on the estate to keep the tradition alive.

By Christmas, Jimmy was crawling; it wasn't long before he was able to pull himself up with the help of his mum. By now he had a full head of curly red hair and was adored by all the estate workers. Cook was particularly fond of him and she spoiled him whenever she had the chance. June still continued to work in the kitchens when they needed her and she sent the extra money to her parents. Her father still hadn't been able to find a permanent job, so they were finding it difficult to cope. Her mother was only too pleased to look after her grandson; at least that way June's father didn't feel that they were living on charity when June sent money. It was June's intention to gradually do more as Jimmy grew up, so she was glad of her mother's help. Both her parents had been impressed when they had first visited the couple's home; they were pleased that she had found someone to look after her so well. Within a few months Jimmy was toddling and keeping his mother on her toes, trying to keep him out of mischief.

Jimmy was a quick learner and was walking before his first birthday. With the help of her mother, June had managed to continue to work in the estate's kitchen. Times were hard, but the Laird and Lady MacCulloch liked to see the young lad around the estate and often gave them all small treats. The estate owners were well aware of the hardships of the less well off and helped when they could. Although things were improving in the more populated towns and cities, the rural areas were taking longer to recover from the effects of the Great Depression. Due to the Laird's kindness, many of the local families had kept their homes, despite not being able to pay rent. Small jobs about the estate were undertaken by those out of work and this helped many to remain in the area. They even found some occasional work for June's father until he managed to find a post nearer to Oban.

June had taken over the care of Brian's hens when they married and loved to watch them as they scratched around in the surrounding grounds. He kept them for the eggs, but also to brood pheasant eggs, which he collected from the wild ones around the estate. The bantams where the best for this, so they had quite a few of these lovely birds. They were June's favourites and she loved their gentle nature. By the time that Jimmy was three, he was helping to collect the eggs. He loved looking for the nests in the hedgerows and the barn. Being small was an advantage when looking under the hedges, as the hens didn't always use the nest boxes in the hen house. Each evening, June and Jimmy would round up the birds and shut them in the hen house to protect them from the foxes. Jimmy was able to pick up the bantams and carry them. His father laughed at the

Point the Finger of Blame

smug look on his son's face as he carried one of the small birds and put it inside for the night. Their neighbour had a couple of nanny goats and Jimmy would stroke them through the fence. They had some of the milk in exchange for some eggs, and of course they had the rabbits, so they always had plenty to eat and drink.

The family had a busy but happy life and, when they could, June and Jimmy would go out for a walk with Brian. By the time Jimmy was school age, he already knew an awful lot about the nature around him, including most of the names of the birds, animals and plants. June and Brian soon decided that, due to the hard times, they would keep their family small. So, Jimmy grew up as an only child. He loved the big open spaces and, when the time came for his first day at school, he didn't want to go. June had difficulty in getting him anywhere near the school building but, once there, Miss English (the Schoolmistress) took him by the hand and led him inside. The school was a small simple building owned by the estate and most of the children came from estate families. Miss English liked to find out as much as she could about the children before they started school, so she was well aware that Jimmy was used to being outside most of the time. She thought he might have difficulties in settling in to the more sedentary life of a classroom. The school had fifteen pupils aged between five and eleven. Jimmy already knew Percy and Rose well, as they lived in one of the cottages close to the Laird's house. Rose was the nearest to Jimmy's age, so Miss English sat Jimmy next to her in the classroom.

DEREK SMITH

Jimmy's desk was by the window and from his seat he could see Glen Lowen and the mountain beyond. He knew the mountain was Benn Ghais; it made him feel more at home to be able to see the beautiful scenery that he was used to being out in. Jimmy gradually settled into his new life, he wasn't the brightest of boys but, if anything caught his interest, he was a quick learner. He had good eye-hand co-ordination and was soon being picked first for sports teams. He was brilliant at cricket and could throw a ball with deadly accuracy. Before long, Jimmy developed a skill with a catapult made from an elastic band, but this new skill soon got him into trouble with Miss English. His first run-in happened when he started to soak the blotting paper in ink and, using the catapult, aimed it at one of the boys in the front row. But just as he fired, the boy dropped his pen and bent down to pick it up. The ink-laden missile missed its target and landed on Miss English's desk, leaving a trail of ink across her papers. When Miss English turned round from the blackboard and saw the mess, she was not amused.

'Who is responsible for this mess?' She looked around the room but Jimmy kept quiet.

'Well, if no one is going to tell me, you can all stay in at playtime until I know who is responsible.'

Everyone let out a groan, but Jimmy kept silent. After a couple of minutes one of the girls spoke out.

'It was Jimmy McLeod miss.'

Miss English walked down the row of desks until she was by Jimmy's side. Looking down at him she could see his ink-stained fingers immediately.

'Go to the front of the class.'

Point the Finger of Blame

Jimmy walked to the front of the room and stood as Miss English approached. She looked very stern and he wondered what was coming. Jimmy was wearing short trousers; she bent slightly and gave Jimmy's leg several hard slaps across the thigh, leaving red marks across his leg. Jimmy stood still and didn't make any noise but he had tears in his eyes. Trying hard to stop himself from crying, he stood there, waiting to see what would happen next; he had always been told that big boys don't cry.

'Go back to your desk,' he heard his teacher say. He slowly walked back and sat in his seat. He was sure the other children were laughing at him; that made his punishment even worse. After school he was given a note to take home to his parents.

June was upset that he had misbehaved at school and sent him straight to bed without any tea. He waited for his father to get home. He was expecting to get into even more trouble then but, to his relief, his father didn't say anything to him. Brian thought that he had been punished enough and was secretly pleased the boy had spirit. Jimmy had learnt his lesson for a while and behaved himself for a few weeks but, being a likeable lad, he sometimes managed to escape minor escapades without punishment. He didn't give up with his catapult but limited its use to outside the classroom; however, he wasn't always careful with his choice of target and broke one of the classroom windows one day in the playground. He soon learnt that this was not a clever thing to do when his father gave him a hiding. Brian hadn't been best pleased about having to pay for the new window pane to be fitted.

DEREK SMITH

Things drifted on for a while without Jimmy getting himself into any more trouble. He was very competitive in sport but, when it came to his school work, he was mediocre; he could often be found gazing out the window at the eagles, soaring up in the thermals above the mountain. Miss English moved him from his window seat in an attempt to keep his attention on the blackboard but he still found it difficult to concentrate. As soon as school was over for the day he would run home, find his dad, and go out to the countryside he loved. In the school holidays his mother could never find him; from dawn to dusk he was outside watching the wildlife and helping his father. Brian was happy that his son showed a love of the wild places and hoped that one day he would take over as the estate's gamekeeper. When June did get time with her son, she took him and his friends down to the loch for a picnic and a paddle at the water's edge. She also taught them all to swim. June knew that they wouldn't be able to resist the water and wanted them to be safe, although she did warn them about going in the water when they were by themselves. Sometimes, Brian would join them with Percy and Rose's parents and they would all have a great time. None of them had ever had a holiday but it didn't worry them; they had all they wanted right on their doorsteps and, besides, except for the Laird they didn't know anyone who did have holidays. It was very much the case of what you've never had you never miss.

Brian was proud of the way his son was growing up. Yes he had been in trouble a couple of times but that was normal: he wouldn't want his son to be otherwise. He showed spirit and that was always good in a lad. Jimmy had a keen interest in his environment and Brian bragged to anyone who would listen that one day Jimmy would be the best gamekeeper in Scotland. Jimmy's enthusiasm for the nature meant that he was out with his father every weekend; he never had to be asked and was keen to learn everything he could. In the spring, he helped to find the pheasants' eggs in the wild so that his father could raise them with the broody hens for the shooting season. This meant that more chicks survived than would have done so in the wild. Jimmy was out on the estate every chance he got; he knew where to find the foxes, badgers, hawks and eagles. He also learnt all he could about guns and loved talking to Mr Baker, the gunsmith, when his father took him into town to buy more cartridges for the guns. Brian only hoped that, when the time came, he would be able to find an under-keeper's job before going on to be a gamekeeper. He passed on as much knowledge as he could to his son to help prepare him for that day. Ideally, he would like Jimmy to get a job on the estate but nothing was certain in life.

By the time Jimmy was eight, World War Two had broken out, and the boys spent a lot of their spare time talking about the bombing rains to the Scottish shipyards. At night, they were able to see the faint glow of the fires caused by the incendiary bombs as they landed. The boys in class soon made up more and more exaggerated stories as they tried to outdo each other, each one claiming to have seen more of the bombers shot down than the others. Due to his occupation, Brian had not been called up to serve in the forces, but June's dad had been drafted to work in the shipyards. Although too old to serve in the army, he was fit enough for the important task of boat building.

June worried about her father but tried not to pass on her fears to her son. Jimmy got on really well with his grandparents and loved it when they visited the estate. However, he didn't like going to Oban on rare visits to them as he hated the closeness of the houses to each other, as well as the fact that he couldn't go out in the countryside.

By the age of ten, Jimmy made his own contribution to the war effort by going out with his ferrets and catching rabbits after school and every weekend. Many local families benefited from the extra meat and he became a firm favourite. The Laird knew what Jimmy was doing but he turned a blind eye; rationing was affecting everyone, including his family. In fact, the Laird's own family and kitchen benefitted from the extra supplies. From the stories Jimmy heard from his granddad on his short and infrequent visits home, Jimmy realised that the town folk were even worse off for food. So, he always made sure his granddad had a couple of rabbits to take back for both his grandmother and his granddad's landlady near the dockyard.

At the age of eleven, Jimmy was to start big school in Oban; his father had brought him a second hand bike but it needed new tyres and these were hard to come by. They had been lucky; one of the local shop owners had just had a delivery before the war and had been very careful to keep some for the local children, as they all had to use bikes to get to the school in Oban. It was one of the community's best kept secrets. He could already ride a bike as Miss English had taught all her pupils to ride on an old bike she kept at the school. Brian warned Jimmy that the bike was only to be used for the school run and nothing else, as he would have

Point the Finger of Blame

difficulty in replacing the tyres or repairing the bike should it get damaged. For once, Jimmy did as he was told. He was proud of his bike and knew that if he wrecked it he wouldn't get another; he didn't fancy walking to and from school. He still found school difficult and wanted to make sure he could get home as soon as he could each day. He hated his new school even more than he had the junior school. It was on the outskirts of Oban but, even so, it had lots of buildings around it. He couldn't wait for the bell to sound at the end of each day so that he could get on his bike and get out into the country air.

Jimmy still got himself into trouble occasionally but the next real episode occurred one playtime. One of the older boys was provoked by his mates to pick a fight with Jimmy. Jimmy wouldn't back away and stood his ground; he retaliated, giving the other boy a bloody nose. They were stopped by one of the teachers who took the pair to the Headmaster, Mr McGill. After listening to both sides of the story, he turned and went to the cupboard at the corner of the room and got out a bamboo cane. Both boys looked at each other. The cane was very bendy but that gave neither boy much cheer as they had heard about the cane and knew that it would hurt.

The Headmaster walked up to Jimmy. 'Hold out your left hand.'

Jimmy held out his hand and the headmaster hit him three times across the palm.

'Now the right hand.'

He hit him three more times. He was unable to move his fingers for a minute or two but still managed not to cry. This was more than the elder boy did; he was still crying as they left the office. Jimmy found that the other lads gave him more respect after that incident as not many boys had the cane without crying. But, his hands hurt for several days and he was upset that he had got into trouble even though he hadn't been the one to start the trouble.

Things seemed to be a bit better after that but he still hated school. A couple of months later, he skived off school one day and spent the day out in the wilds. However, his parents found out and grounded him for a week, not letting him go out and about on the estate once he got home. To him this was worse than being caned; he never skipped school again.

That summer holiday the Laird's nephew, Jonathan, came to stay at the big house. He was shortly to start boarding school. His father was a naval officer and his mother had been asked to help in the naval control room at one of the bases in Scotland. So the Laird had offered to look after him in the holidays. Wanting to be with children his own age, Jonathan had asked if he could play with the estate workers' children. The Laird and his wife readily agreed as they felt it important that Jonathan have company during his stay. They themselves had never had children and one day the estate would be Jonathan's, so they felt it important for him to have some understanding of it.

So Jonathan was introduced to Jimmy, Percy and Rose by his uncle. The group set off for a picnic of jam sandwiches and a small cake that each had scavenged from the cook as a treat. Although Jonathan was the same age as Jimmy, he was much taller and stronger; this was something Jimmy was used to as he had always been smaller than most of the youngsters his

Point the Finger of Blame

age. This had only made him more determined to prove himself; something that had got him into trouble more than once.

The children walked down to the loch edge and began to play hide and seek. This soon progressed to climbing trees; something than Jimmy excelled at as his slim build allowed him to scramble through spaces between branches that Jonathan couldn't get through with his bigger frame. After a while, the boys decided to have a stone throwing contest. Rose was given the job of sticking some sticks into the ground like cricket stumps. There were plenty of pebbles on the ground and the three boys had soon selected those that they felt were the best for throwing. Percy stepped out twenty two paces and threw his jumper down to mark the spot. Percy threw first and missed; Jonathan went next and hit the middle stick out of the ground. It was now Jimmy's turn and he also knocked over the middle stick. This meant that Percy was knocked out and Jonathan and Jimmy prepared to throw again. Moving the jumper back a further ten paces to make it more of a challenge the boys threw once more. Jonathan was first to throw and missed all the sticks. Jimmy grinned to himself; this was going to be easy. Throwing his first pebble he hit the middle stick out once more and quickly threw two more pebbles, knocking the other two sticks out of the ground. He jumped up in the air and cheered in victory. Jonathan was a poor loser and made all sorts of excuses for his poor showing. Percy tried to calm things down, pointing out that he hadn't hit any at all. Percy winked at Jimmy; he knew he hadn't stood a chance having played with Jimmy before. Rose shouted at them to come and have the picnic which she had set out by the loch's edge, using a fallen tree as a table. The food made the boys settle down and on the walk back home they soon became friends again.

The summer holidays flew past. Jimmy taught Jonathan how to catch rabbits using the ferrets and they swam in the loch on the hotter days. At the end of the holidays the Laird invited them all to the house for tea. It was a sunny day and they sat out on the veranda overlooking the neatly cut lawns. They had sandwiches, cream buns and fruit cakes all washed down with apple juice from the orchard. Rose, Percy and Jimmy had never eaten as well. Lady MacCulloch had asked the cook to make the day special so quite a few rations had been saved. After they had finished all the food they had a game of croquet on the lawn, the hoops had already been set out and the mallet and balls lay neatly on the path.

Of the children, only Jonathan knew how to play, but Lady MacCulloch soon told the other three the rudiments of the game. Jonathan won the first game easily and was very pleased with himself. But Jimmy soon got the grasp of the skills needed and won the second game. Thinking it was beginners luck, Jonathan talked Lady MacCulloch into letting them have another game. Deciding they had enough time, Lady MacCulloch agreed. Jimmy went on to easily win this game as well. With that, Jonathan threw his mallet to the ground and stomped off indoors. Rose, Percy and Jimmy collected the hoops, mallets and balls and packed them away. They thanked Lady MacCulloch for the lovely tea.

Point the Finger of Blame

Turning to walk away, the trio were called back by Lady MacCulloch. 'Don't forget this.' She was holding out a package containing the remains of their picnic.

Thanking her again, they set off home; they were unable to resist the food and it was all devoured by the time they got home.

CHAPTER THREE

With the holiday over, the children had to return to school. Jimmy enjoyed his cycle rides each day but still found being in the classroom far less exciting than being outside. His progress was average except in sports, where he excelled. His competitive spirit made him difficult to beat.

The tide of the war had turned once the Americans had joined the allies. Unlike some areas, there were no Americans stationed nearby, so Jimmy never got to meet any of them. His life continued much as before until he reached the age of thirteen, when the war finally ended. There were many parties to celebrate and the men that had left to fight drifted back to the estate. Many families had lost members, so although everyone was pleased the war was over; there was much sadness for those who did not return. Life gradually settled down to normal once more. Although rationing continued for another nine years, it didn't affect Jimmy too much, as the family always had enough food due to the constant supply of rabbit and pigeon. He had never been used to a lot of the things that were on ration and his parents had a good vegetable garden.

Point the Finger of Blame

One day, Jimmy came back home after visiting the loch and found his father training the gun dogs in a small paddock at the side of the house. Jimmy knew not to disturb his dad but he had seen something important that he wanted to share, so he went and found his mother. June was making dinner in the kitchen. Hearing her son come in the door, she turned toward him with a smile on her face. He quickly told his mum what he had seen and, as soon as his father came in, June asked Jimmy to tell his dad what he had told her.

Jimmy turned to his dad; he was a bit nervous as he hoped he wasn't going to seem silly.

'Come on boy, what have you got to say?'

Jimmy burst out: 'Down at the loch there's something you ought to see. I've never seen anything like it before.'

Brian was curious and, not even waiting for his tea or to ask what it was he said: 'Come on then son, let's go and see what it is.'

Jimmy's mother wanted to go as well, so they waited whilst she pulled the dinner to the side of the range and got her coat. Then they all set off to the loch. Jimmy grabbed his binoculars off the side where they were kept and followed his parents as they left the house.

Once they got about one hundred yards from the loch, Jimmy turned to his father and said: 'See that willow tree at the water's edge, the one that is going hollow with age?'

Brian looked toward the willows. There were several at the water's edge, they were coppiced by the local thatcher for spars. Then he immediately saw the one his son was referring to.

'There's a hollow half way up the trunk and another nearer the top. The lower hollow has a duck's nest in it and if you look at the one above, it has a tawny owl's nest in it.'

He was right. Brian had never seen the like before. He turned to Jimmy.

'Well spotted son. I expect the ducklings will fledge before the owl chicks arrive. That might give them the chance to survive, but why the duck stayed there I don't understand. Unless her eggs were already laid before the tawny chose her nest hole.'

Jimmy was so pleased he had spotted something even his father hadn't seen before. After his mum had a look, they all set off home for their meal. They were still talking about the strange site as they ate their food. Brian was once again pleased at how well his son's observational skills were progressing. He wasn't sure that he would have noticed the two nests.

For the next couple of weeks Jimmy kept a close eye on the nests and, as his dad predicted, the ducklings fledged before the owl chicks hatched. There had been twelve ducklings but only six survived. Maybe the tawny owl caught them or perhaps it was one of the pikes in the loch. He would never know. Two of the three tawny owl chicks also survived, but the loss of chicks was nature's way and he knew he couldn't do anything about it. All the creatures need to feed their young and, in most cases, some other creature has to lose some of their offspring as a result. He had learnt at a young age to accept such things.

When not at school Jimmy spent many hours with his dad out on the estate. Brian taught his son how to shoot and was amazed at his progress; Jimmy had a

Point the Finger of Blame

natural talent and was soon hitting most of what he aimed at. Jimmy was also taught, at the same time, how to care for guns and make sure they were always safe to use. In fact, the first thing he learnt was never to leave a gun loaded and never to point it, even an unloaded one, at anyone.

When Jimmy reached fifteen, it was time for him to leave school. Brian, realising his son's love of guns, asked John Baker, the local gunsmith, if he had a place for his son. He was disappointed that there was no place at present but acknowledged that the returning men needed the jobs more. The Laird said that he was unable to take on another gamekeeper but Brian still hoped that the Laird would allow Jimmy to join him once things settled down and returned to normal. John Baker had known Brian for many years and, having met Jimmy many times on his father's visits to the shop, agreed that he could help him set up the targets for an Army Cadet competition at the local Territorial Army practice range; this way, John could judge for himself whether Jimmy would work well in his small firm.

He knew that Brian would have taught his son about guns but wanted to judge the lad's nature for himself before agreeing to give him a job.

Jimmy was up bright and early on the day of the competition; he ate his breakfast and cycled up to Mr Baker's shop. He helped load up the van with the guns and other equipment before setting off to the ranges. They soon had the targets set up and had marked out the lines; it wasn't long before some of the T.A. arrived to erect the tents for the judges. Then, the cadets started to arrive. Mr Baker told Jimmy that most of the cadets were hoping to go onto The Royal Military

Academy at Sandhurst. Jimmy was surprised to see the Laird's nephew Jonathan was with the group from Merchiston Castle School.

'Stop gawking Jimmy and lets finish our work, you'll have plenty of time to look around once we're set up,' came Mr Baker's voice.

Jimmy turned around to see Mr Baker walking toward the firing lines.

'We need to try out the targets to make sure they're working okay.'

With that, Jimmy's attention was instantly back on the job at hand. There was a bunker beneath the two targets. The targets were human shaped and painted to look like German soldiers: a leftover from the recent war. Each of the targets had a series of rings painted over the position where a human heart would be. There were three rings of varying colours, each smaller than the last, with a black bulls-eye in the centre. Jimmy went down into the bunker and hoisted up the targets with a rope, shouting when he was in a safe position so that Mr Baker knew he could commence shooting. Picking up a 303 rifle, Mr Baker shot four times at the targets. Once he had finished firing he called out to Jimmy, who lowered the targets to check for the results. There were three bulls-eyes and one in the inner ring. Using the walky-talky, he told Mr Baker the results. Satisfied with the results, Mr Baker informed the organisers that the competition could begin.

There were quite a few spectators and the guests of honour were the Laird and his wife, who had been accompanied to the site by Jimmy's father, who was to enter the gamekeeper's challenge. The day's competition was soon underway. The shooting was of a

Point the Finger of Blame

high standard and very competitive. Jimmy wasn't surprised when his father won his section. Brian received a ten pound prize as well as a small cup. The cadet competition followed and Jonathan won his section, the Laird was obviously very proud of his nephew as he presented him with his cup. It was then announced that before the under-eighteen final any of the local lads present could have a small competition of their own. Jimmy jumped at the chance, not realising that Mr Baker had asked if this could take place. Mr Baker knew from Brian that Jimmy was a good shot but he wanted to see how he would cope under pressure. There were a group of about twenty boys present, but only six stepped forward to try their luck. None of the boys had ever fired a 303 before but they were all determined to do their best. As this was an unplanned round they each fired six shots and the winner was the boy with the highest score. It didn't take long for Jimmy to get used to the gun and he easily won. The Laird donated five pounds as the prize and Jimmy was as proud as punch as he stepped up to receive it.

The winners of the under-eighteen groups gathered to start the final. The cadets' leader asked Jimmy if he would like to take part, even though he had little experience of the gun. Jimmy agreed instantly. He was offered the chance of a handicap but refused; his competitive nature would not let him concede that he needed any help.

The final consisted of three rounds of knockouts and it was soon clear that the two finalists would be Jonathan and Jimmy. Each of the boys was to have five shots, Jonathan won the toss and shot first, he hit the bull. Jimmy stepped forward and took careful aim. His first shot was also a bull. Each of the boys' following three shots were bulls, so with one shot each to go it was neck and neck. The crowd fell completely silent as Jonathan took aim. His fifth shot was just outside the bull. Tension mounted but Jimmy remained calm. Taking careful aim he fired, he knew that he had hit the bull. The judges announced the bull and the crowd roared. It had been an exciting final. Jonathan turned to Jimmy, holding out his hand.

'Well done Jimmy.'

Although Jimmy could see Jonathan was disappointed, he had obviously done some growing up and showed no sign of the spoilt child of his youth. The day had been a great one for Jimmy; he had fifteen pounds prize money in his pocket and Mr Baker gave him a job on the spot. Life couldn't be better.

CHAPTER FOUR

Jimmy loved his new job and Mr Baker found him a quick learner; his love of guns and all things connected with them shone through in everything he did. Working six days a week, Jimmy didn't get a chance to see his old school friends much. Before long, Percy tried to enlist in the army but was unsuccessful, so he moved away from the area to stay with his uncle. Jimmy later heard that his old friend had started work in the coal mines. Jimmy couldn't imagine a worse job, away from the sunlight, but he wished his childhood friend all the best. Rose had met a Canadian who had joined the Royal Air Force for the war. The couple had married, then moved to Canada. Jimmy had always looked on Percy and Rose as the siblings he'd never had and was sorry to see them both go. They had promised to keep in touch before they all went their separate ways. Having few other close friends he spent most of his spare time with his father when not at work, although he did see Jonathan from time to time.

Mr Baker was a very strict man; he told Jimmy from the very first day that he must treat anything to do with guns as dangerous.

DEREK SMITH

'You must check and double check everything. I know you are used to guns and your father has said you are careful and obey all his rules but you will find assembling and repairing guns is a different matter and you need to learn the ways of the workshop.'

He paused and looked at Jimmy, as if to ensure he was being listened to.

'I understand sir,' Jimmy replied.

He found Mr Baker a bit intimidating at first but soon realised that, as long as he did as he was told and showed interest, Mr Baker was a great teacher.

The workshop was at the back of the shop and had a bell over the door that rang whenever anyone entered. This meant that they could concentrate on their work without having to keep an eye on the front of shop. They worked in silence, except when Mr Baker was giving Jimmy instructions on how to do the various tasks he was given. This suited Jimmy as he found it easier to concentrate this way. At first he was taught how to use the many different files and which file to use for which job. There were a confusing number of them all in a rack on the wall. It took Jimmy months to learn the correct ones to use. He got told off more than once for using the wrong one, but this helped him to learn. Mr Baker was secretly pleased with Jimmy's progress.

From the very beginning Mr Baker had said that he wouldn't be giving Jimmy an apprenticeship as he would teach him all he knew as they went along. Jimmy was happy with this as it meant he got paid a bit more. His pay wasn't great; he got fifteen shillings a week, but he wasn't accustomed to getting any money so it was more than he was used to.

Point the Finger of Blame

'Stick at it lad,' his father had told him when he took his first pay packet home. 'You won't regret it; whatever you end up doing, knowing about guns is always a useful trade.'

Mr Baker sold everything to do with country pursuits in his shop, as well as a range of army surplus left over from the war. He had a selection of camouflage jackets and some good binoculars that Jimmy had his eye on. But he knew they would have to wait for a while. Once he had paid his mother for his keep and replaced some of his working clothes, he wouldn't have any spare cash for some time.

One Saturday morning, Jimmy turned up at work as normal but, when he went into the shop, he found Mr Baker all dressed up in his suit.

'Jimmy, I've got to go and deliver Laird McGrew's Purdy over to Glen Nevis so I'm closing the shop for the day. As it's short notice, you can have the day off with full pay. But mind you get here first thing Monday morning.'

'Thank you sir,' said Jimmy with a big grin on his face. He had been working for Mr Baker for several months now and this was his first extra day off. He couldn't believe his luck.

With that, rather than catch the bus home, he went further down Oban high street. He decided that he would spend the day getting some new working clothes for himself; he was in need of a new pair of trousers as his mother had already mended his present trousers several times and they were beginning to look decidedly the worse for wear. At midday he went into a café where he knew youngsters of the area hung out. He knew some of them from school and soon got talking to a few of the lads. Sitting at the next table were four giggling girls; he recognised them from his school days but hadn't seen them for ages; that didn't stop one of them coming across and speaking to him.

'Hi, you're Jimmy McLeod aren't you?'

He nodded his head, but before he had a chance to say any more she continued.

'I wondered if you would like to take me to see *Gone with the Wind* at the pictures; all my friends are going and I've no one to go with.'

Jimmy jumped at the chance. 'Okay, but when does it start? My last bus leaves at ten thirty.'

'At half past six, so you'll have plenty of time.'

'Right, I'll meet you outside the pictures at six o'clock then. It's Mary, isn't it?'

The girl nodded, going red as if embarrassed by what she had just done.

She quickly spoke: 'See you there then,' and then ran off to join her friends.

A couple of the lads teased him about what had happened but Jimmy took no notice.

He made his way to the bus station and caught the next bus home. He would have plenty of time to get ready before catching it back. Jimmy thought the timing was perfect as the bus would get him back to Oban just before six o'clock.

That evening he went back to town all spruced up and walked from the bus station to the cinema, getting there in plenty of time. He was feeling rather pleased with himself. It was the first time he had been out with a girl on a date. After meeting up with her, he found that he had to pay for both of them to go in to see the film; he also paid for their ice creams in the interval: it was

Point the Finger of Blame

going to be an expensive evening for him. They were sat in the back row and held hands. When the film got to one of the weepy bits, Mary put her head on his shoulder. Not quite sure what to do, he half-heartedly put his arm around her shoulder and she snuggled in closer. Once the film finished they walked outside and, as soon as they got to the door, Mary's father stepped forward.

'Hope you enjoyed the film,' he said, looking at the pair.

That solved Jimmy's dilemma. He had been wondering whether he should give Mary a kiss before he went home but it was obvious that wasn't going to happen with her father stood there.

'See you the same time next week Jimmy and thank you for a lovely evening.'

With that, Mary turned and walked off down the pavement with her father.

Jimmy stood there for a few moments before turning and walking to the bus stop.

The couple met up for the next four weeks and the arm around the shoulder gradually became a gentle kiss. On a couple of occasions, Mary kissed him with her mouth open. Jimmy found that strange and wasn't sure how to react. He was walking on air and couldn't wait for Saturdays to come round. All his small savings were disappearing and he had no idea when he would be able to afford his binoculars. All his spare money was being spent on their nights at the pictures. Mary had a job in Woolworths but never offered to pay for anything. Jimmy didn't care.

CHAPTER FIVE

At work, Mr Baker was very pleased with how Jimmy was progressing and let him replace the barrels of a twelve bore shotgun. Jimmy looked at the old one; there was a bulge about four inches from the end. Mr Baker explained that this could happen if the gun wasn't cleaned after use.

'The barrel gets pitted and thin, and then if something, even as light as a spider's web, is in the barrel when the gun is fired, it will cause pressure to build up and push on the weak spots.'

Jimmy looked up the barrel and could see the pits; he understood now why his father always insisted on guns being cleaned carefully after they were used and before anything else was done. He felt that he was learning such a lot and all sorts of things were becoming clearer to him. It was quite late on Friday by the time Jimmy finished replacing the barrel. But he was pleased with what he had done and set off home in good spirits.

The next morning Mr Baker checked the gun over and was satisfied with the standard of work.

Point the Finger of Blame

'As it's only just down the road, you can deliver the gun to Mr Martin. He lives in the last house at the end of the street. Put the gun in its case, lad.'

Jimmy picked up the leather case from the side. He knew the case was called a leg of mutton as it looked a bit like a large leg joint. He thought it made him look like he was carrying a musical instrument.

To get to Mr Martin's house, he had to pass the café where he had first met Mary. It was always busy on a Saturday and, as he walked toward the café, a motorbike pulled up and stopped. There was a girl on the bike, riding pillion and showing some bare thigh above her stockings. The couple dismounted the bike and stood by the side of it, passionately kissing each other, without worrying who could see them. As Jimmy got closer, he recognised Mary. At first he couldn't believe what he was seeing and was then really hurt that she could do such a thing. He walked briskly past and delivered the gun to Mr Martin. By the time he got back there was no sign of the couple, although the bike was still parked outside the café. He walked quickly passed the window with his eyes straight ahead.

Once he got back, he started working back at his bench. He wasn't concentrating on his work and found himself being told off a couple of times by Mr Baker. Once he had finished work he went straight home, still mulling over what he had seen. Later that day, he had arranged to see Mary as usual but instead he collected up his fishing gear and went off down to the loch. This gave Jimmy the time to think; he always found he did his best thinking when sitting with a rod in his hand. He decided that girls were too expensive for him and that he had obviously misread the signals he had been getting from Mary. He had begun to feel very fond of her and had thought she felt the same way but, if he couldn't trust his judgement with women, he would leave them well alone and not bother with them. His parents had realised he'd been seeing a girl but had not pressed him on the matter, so when he stopped going into Oban every Saturday or Sunday evening they just assumed the romance had petered out. He was a young man and they were sure he would find someone else in time. So they never raised the subject with him.

Jimmy threw himself into his work and learnt all he could from Mr Baker. It wasn't long before Mr Baker was happy to leave Jimmy to repair the guns that came into the shop and assemble new ones with only minimal supervision. Jimmy was always willing to ask if he needed advice and that was good enough for Mr Baker. They spent long hours working together and Jimmy soaked up knowledge like a sponge. The pair worked well together and enjoyed the companionship that their shared interest gave them. Mr Baker was pleased that at long last he had found someone who was genuinely interested in the job and he didn't regret his decision to employ Jimmy.

Not only that, but Jimmy was now able to save up all his spare money, and soon had enough to buy the binoculars and camouflage jacket he had wanted. Mr Baker had also given him a pay rise and he was now getting one pound ten shillings a week. He liked nothing better than to spend his spare time helping his father with the estate shoots and fishing groups; this meant that, by the time he was eighteen, he was a very good marksman. Just after his eighteenth birthday he received his call up papers for his National Service. Mr

Point the Finger of Blame

Baker was sorry to see him go as they had worked well together but he knew he had no choice. He told Jimmy to look him up when he came back and if there was a job going he would gladly take him back.

A week later, he travelled to Oban for his medical and, having been passed as fit, he only had a week at home before travelling by train to Glasgow. Nearing Glasgow, he was amazed at its size, having never been anywhere larger than Oban. As the train pulled into the station, he looked out the window; he thought it a dirty and noisy city, not understanding how anyone would want to live there. The crowds on the platforms seemed huge to Jimmy as he moved through them and joined the other young men, waiting at the station collection point. It wasn't long before they were all put into the back of trucks to make the journey to the barracks. They were crammed in together on wooden benches, each clutching a suitcase. None of them spoke at first, each one wondering what was in store for them. The back of the truck was filled with tension until one of the lads farted; as with young men everywhere, this caused some nervous laughter and caused holding of noses and other comments. The ice was broken and the lads were soon swapping names and cracking jokes. The convoy of trucks went through the streets of Glasgow and Jimmy and some of the other country lads couldn't believe that people actually chose to live in such an environment. But they soon stopped looking out the back of the truck and, by the time they reached the barracks, they were all singing together. Jimmy had never experienced anything like it before; he felt as if they were no longer individuals but had pulled together and were set to make the most of the situation they found themselves in.

The camp was set out in the countryside not far from Glasgow and consisted of a series of wooden and tin huts, like so many others that were scattered across the country. The group started their ten week basic training as soon as they had settled into their respective huts. It didn't take long for the lads in each hut to become friends. They were soon working as a team and the days were filled with marching, cleaning and rifle practice. They spent nights out in the local countryside learning how to conduct themselves in battle situations. At the rifle ranges Jimmy's talent soon became obvious; he was by far the best shot of the group. When one of the other lad's guns jammed, the sergeant ordered the gun to be returned to the armourer; overhearing this, Jimmy offered to sort it out on the spot but this didn't go down very well with the sergeant.

'Shut up McLeod. I give the orders, if I wanted you to do anything I'd have asked you. Nobody tinkers with jammed guns but the armourer, until I say otherwise,' the sergeant shouted.

Jimmy made the fatal error of looking like he was going to speak again. Before he said a word the sergeant glared at him.

'Cook house duties for you this weekend; your pass is to be handed in.'

The young lad whose gun had jammed looked upset and was just about to say something when the lad stood next to him jabbed him in the ribs and whispered: 'Shut up or you will catch it as well.'

So, he kept his mouth firmly shut.

Point the Finger of Blame

Once they got out of the sergeant's earshot, he went up to Jimmy and apologised for being the reason he had got in to trouble.

'Don't worry, it wasn't your fault, I should have known better. Go and enjoy yourself and have a drink for me.'

Despite what he had said, Jimmy was upset. After six weeks training he had been looking forward to a night out with the lads; they had planned to go to the local town and unwind; it was obvious that he needed to be more careful in future before speaking out. He had enjoyed getting to know the lads better; they had all bonded well and by now several had nicknames, some of which were quite funny. They had all been looking forward to letting their hair down and having fun after their experience of basic training. Over the weeks they had formed a brotherhood, looking after each other and trying to avoid the worst of the Sergeant Major's bullying. The other lads were disappointed that Jimmy would not be joining them but this didn't stop them looking forward to their leave.

The next morning, as the group set off to the nearby town, Jimmy reported to the cookhouse. As he had anticipated, he was given the worst jobs to do and spent the first part of his shift spud-bashing. He was sick of the sight of potatoes by the time he had finished peeling several sacks of the vegetables. But his day got worse as he then had to clean all the pans used by the cooks that morning and lunchtime. One of the other lads told him that when someone was sent as punishment to the kitchens, the cooks deliberately left the pans over the heat once the food was removed, to burn the food residue hard. Jimmy could well believe this as it took him ages to clean the pans to the satisfaction of the cooks. His hands were raw in places by the time he had finished; although he was well used to hard work, having his hands in water had softened them, causing the skin to break in places. Jimmy found the work soul-destroying, not only was he missing his leave, but he hated the work he was being made to do and the deliberate burning of the pots left him feeling unduly put upon. But his pride stopped him from showing just how much he hated doing what he had been told to do. After all, he had only been trying to help out. A saying he'd heard his grandfather use came to mind: 'You do the crime, you do the time.'

After he had finished the washing up, the head cook took pity on him. Jimmy had done all that was given to him to do without a word of complaint, so he was allowed to return to his billet. With nothing better to do, he put on the radio to listen to the news. The main news story was about Korea. It appeared that North Korea was preparing to invade South Korea; the United Nations was warning North Korea that it would not tolerate this aggressive act against another state and it would support the South Koreans if this continued. The reporter said the general feeling was that the situation would progress to conflict. Jimmy was stunned by the thought, he hadn't been in the army long and it looked like he might become involved in a war situation. He hoped that sense would prevail and the North Koreans would back down from open conflict with their neighbours. Listening to the news had lowered his mood even further; with all his mates out having fun he lay down on his bunk and tried to sleep.

Point the Finger of Blame

Just as he had begun to doze off, in came the sergeant of the guard. Jimmy jumped up and stood to attention.

'Stand at ease McLeod, I've come to take you to the Commanding Officer.'

Jimmy was wondering what he had done but thought it best not to ask. He quickly followed the sergeant as he marched to the C.O.s office at the other end of the camp. As they entered the office he saw his commanding officer, Captain McGee, together with a general and a major sitting at the desk. Jimmy started to feel very worried; what had he done to be called before such a group? He quickly stood to attention and saluted, staring ahead. Captain McGee returned his salute, giving Jimmy a friendly smile he pointed to a chair.

'Sit down McLeod.'

Jimmy sat down opposite the three officers; the sergeant stood at the door behind him. Despite the smile from the Captain, Jimmy continued to feel very apprehensive. He couldn't help but think back to a war film he had watched just before he started his training, where the hero sat before three German officers before being dragged out and shot.

'Relax young man.'

The General's voice cut through Jimmy's thoughts.

'You're not in any trouble, quite the opposite; Captain McGee has been monitoring your progress and, apart from the incident which resulted in your pass being revoked, he has been very impressed with you. Particularly your ability to shoot; also, your survival crafts are excellent.'

Pausing before continuing, the General looked at Jimmy as if trying to make up his mind about something. .

'We feel that your natural abilities and talents might be better used by the army if you became a sniper. To be a sniper for your battalion, you have to be a volunteer; we can't make you do this. This post requires a man with nerves of steel and involves special training. A sniper has to live and fight behind enemy lines. You would have to prove your toughness, intelligence, and suitability, as both your life and your battalion's safety would depend on your actions.'

The General paused before continuing. 'We are giving you a week to consider volunteering for this role. As of now you are on a week's leave. You will be taken home in the morning by Captain McGee's staff car and collected again next Sunday. I will tell you this as food for thought: a sniper is someone who gains the respect of all those who come into contact with him. He is trained to be self sufficient in all things, including armed and unarmed combat. He never boasts of his position and he is in danger twenty-four seven. But his actions can make the difference between life and death for many of his colleagues and in some cases can shorten conflicts.'

He paused for a moment, looking at Jimmy for some sort of reaction.

'Do you understand what is being asked of you?'

Jimmy nodded. For once he was unable to speak; this was the last thing he had expected.

'You're not to speak of this meeting to anyone, not even your family. It is important that you keep this very quiet for reasons I'm not prepared to share with you at

Point the Finger of Blame

this time. If you do talk out of turn, you may find yourself facing a court marshal. There are four of us in this room who will testify that this meeting has never happened, so mum's the word. I cannot stress how important it is for this to remain under wraps at this time. As I said, this post of sniper is voluntary, so think hard about what we have said and consider carefully before making your decision.'

The General paused once more as if thinking.

'All I will say, McLeod, is that if you do decide to volunteer you will be helping your country far more than being among the rank and file, so please give this a great deal of consideration. Thank you for your time, McLeod; enjoy your leave and we hope you make the right decision.'

Jimmy stood up and saluted before turning toward the door. The sergeant marched him back to his billet.

Thinking the sergeant had left, Jimmy turned and put the kettle on. He was stunned by what had just occurred.

'Yes please.' The voice came from behind him. To Jimmy's surprise, he found himself making tea for one of the hated sergeants. His mates wouldn't be very happy if they ever found out. The sergeant took off his hat and sat down. Jimmy made the tea and gave the sergeant a cup before sitting down. The sergeant looked Jimmy straight in the eye and then started to talk.

'I served in the last war McLeod. I've seen firsthand what fear a good enemy sniper can create. I know the hatred we felt against them and the respect we had for them if they got captured. There is nothing to compare with it. Don't expect to be treated as an ordinary soldier;

if you do become a sniper you'll be apart, not one of the boys. Before you decide, give it plenty of thought. If you refuse nobody will think any less of you, none of your mates will ever know.'

The sergeant took a deep breath before continuing. 'Don't allow yourself to feel any pressure to volunteer, if you don't think it's right for you don't do it. You're not a career soldier so you don't need to impress anyone.'

The sergeant paused and sipped his tea, as if making a decision. Looking at Jimmy, he took a big breath and continued.

'This is the biggest decision of your life, McLeod. I know what I'm talking about; I was a sniper in the last war. It's a lonely life. I was bayoneted when caught in France and left for dead; lucky for me the Germans were on the run and I was found in time and saved. I was brought home. I expect you've noticed I never join in the strenuous exercises or physical activities.'

With this, he pulled up his shirt. Jimmy could see a deep ugly scar that ran across the sergeant's abdomen.

'The army looks after its own. They nursed me back to health and because of my previous duties they allowed me to stay in the army and have kept me on light duties ever since. I was one of the lucky ones. Don't let me put you off, but you need to know what you're letting yourself in for if you agree. Remember, it won't be the General out there on his own facing danger every minute, but you.'

After readjusting his clothing, he turned and left the billet. Jimmy realised that his opinion of the sergeant had changed after what he had just learnt. He found himself admiring the man in a way he never expected to.

CHAPTER SIX

Jimmy didn't sleep much that night; he had too much to think about. So when the staff car arrived early the next morning, he was packed and waiting. It was a long drive and Jimmy found himself thinking of what had happened; he knew the decision he made might change his life in ways he could only guess at. At the same time, he couldn't help but feel flattered by the fact he had been singled out. As he neared his home, he asked the driver to drop him off. He didn't want his parents to ask awkward questions if he arrived in a staff car. The car pulled over and he got out the car. It soon disappeared out of sight. Jimmy soon walked the last half mile home. Once he reached the back door of his parent's home, he stopped and paused before entering. His mother was stood by the range with her back towards him. He crept up and tapped her on the shoulder. Spinning around, she gasped in surprise when she saw it was her son. She tapped him gently on his top of his head with the wooden spoon she was holding.

'You beast, surprising me like that; when I heard the door open I thought it was your father playing his normal tricks.'

With that she hugged her son, before shouting for her husband who was in the back yard. Jimmy hadn't noticed him as he approached the house; he was in the coal shed getting some more fuel for the range. When he saw his son, Brian's face lit up. He had really missed having Jimmy about.

'Well look what the cat's dragged in.' Brian was grinning from ear to ear. 'Why didn't you tell us you were coming? I'd have met you at the station.'

Dropping his voice to a whisper: 'It would have got me out of going to chapel.'

Jimmy smiled. He had forgotten it was Sunday.

'Sorry, it was a quick decision. I didn't know I was getting leave until the last minute.'

At least that wasn't a lie, thought Jimmy. He wasn't looking forward to keeping the truth from his parents and he wasn't even sure if he could. They had always been able to read him like a book. Jimmy had arrived just in time for the midday meal, so they sat down and caught up with all the news whilst they ate their meal. Jimmy was careful to keep his news brief and made no mention of the latest developments. After lunch, Brian had to go up to the big house for a meeting. The estate manager had called and Jimmy's mother had to go with him as she still worked part-time in the kitchens, so Jimmy took himself off for a long walk.

He didn't realise just how much he'd missed the openness and beauty until he had come back. His time in basic training had been so busy and tiring that he hadn't spent too much time thinking about home. His

Point the Finger of Blame

new friendships had also helped with the transition. Of course he'd missed his parents and often thought of them, but not the wide open spaces and tranquillity. He soon found himself sitting at his father's favourite place, overlooking the valley and lochs. A golden eagle flew overhead and he marvelled at its grace and the ease with which it moved through the air. Although he worked with his father, he had never developed the same feelings of hatred towards the birds of prey that his father had. He knew that the birds took some of the grouse and other game but he had more tolerance of the beautiful birds. In the far distance, a herd of red deer moved though the landscape; the stag at a distance, keeping a wary eye on what he was doing. The deer were well used to the hunting parties that regularly reduced their number; they never trusted humans or allowed them to get too near the herd.

It was quite late by the time Jimmy returned to the house and, after all that had happened to him in the last few days, he decided to have a quick bite to eat and go to bed early. He asked his mum to wake him up when they rose so he could go out with his dad for the day.

The next morning, after a quick breakfast, Jimmy and Brian left the house and went up to the pheasant pens; they checked all the birds after feeding, then went on to check some of the other game on the estate. Brian had several traps to check and reset. Part of his job was to control the vermin on the estate. Lady MacCulloch had been losing several of her favourite plants in the gardens to rabbits and Brian had snared several overnight.

'Come on lad, we'll take these up to the kitchen. I'm sure Cook will use them for the staff dinners later. It will give them all a chance to say hello. They often mention you.'

'I might see if I can see the Laird and Lady MacCulloch whilst we're up at the house.'

Jimmy had always liked the couple who, since he was a young boy, had always been kind to him.

'No point son. They're both in London this week on business, so if you're around here at all keep your eyes on the place.'

The men continued up to the kitchens and delivered the rabbits. As expected, the cook was pleased to relieve them of the welcome addition to the menu. She was pleased that Jimmy was home for a visit, having always had a soft spot for the gamekeeper's son. After spending about half an hour catching up on all the news, the pair went up to the moors. They had lots of catching up to do and Brian was keen to know how Jimmy was finding the army life.

'It's alright. Lots of shooting at targets and marching around the place, but I miss the open spaces and the silence. The lads are a good bunch but they never stop talking, and let's not forget the sergeant majors. They could be heard from one end of the estate to the other!'

Brian laughed. 'I don't suppose for one minute you stay silent for too long either. Now to the important things; tell me what guns you have been using.'

The couple spent the rest of their trip back down to the house talking guns. June had a lunch of bread and cheese ready for them. Brian usually took his with him but he knew June was anxious to see something of their son on his visit, so they had decided on the previous evening that they would both return for their meal. After his meal, Brian went back out. Jimmy spent

Point the Finger of Blame

the next hour with his mother until she had to leave to go to work and then he went out on the moor. The next few days followed a very similar pattern and Jimmy managed to keep his secret. But when he was up on the moor, he spent hours thinking of what to do on his return. He loved shooting and pitting his wits against nature but deliberately shooting his fellow man in cold blood was a different matter; he wasn't sure if he would be able to do it. Jimmy also spent time fishing on the lochs. This gave him the ideal opportunity to think and his mother loved fish so he was happy to oblige her. He had always done his best thinking whilst fishing. Its solitary nature lent itself to deep thought.

One evening the family sat in front of the fire listening to the news on the radio; the continuing unrest between North and South Korea was the headline piece.

Jimmy's mother looked concerned and, turning to Brian, said: 'I hope nothing comes of this. We should have learnt our lesson by now and stopped all this fighting. I wouldn't want our Jimmy to have to go out there.'

'Don't worry, they're only flexing their muscles; they wouldn't dare upset the U.N. With America in the U.N, it's too big for them to fight,' said Brian with a confident tone to his voice.

This seemed to reassure June but Jimmy wasn't as certain. However, he kept his silence. Changing the subject, they spent the rest of the evening playing cards around the table. Jimmy's mother won overall and was quite pleased with herself.

Late the following afternoon, Brian asked Jimmy to help him sort out the growing rabbit and pigeon problem; the numbers of both had been growing of late and needed reducing. Collecting their guns and ammunition, they headed out together. Jimmy found himself a good spot and, sitting quietly in the hedgerow, he waited for the rabbits to emerge. Using his favourite 22 gun, the rabbits were easy targets and he told his dad so; his father laughed.

'What, do you want them to shoot back at you?'

This made Jimmy think once again of the decision he needed to make. He never had trouble killing pests but, if his life was in danger, would he still manage to shoot? Or would he run for it? Well, the rabbits didn't test his courage, nor did the pigeons.

Later that evening, Jimmy was glad when his parents decided on an early night. He told his parents that a staff car was picking him up as the driver was coming past the estate, so he wouldn't need a lift to the station the next morning. Jimmy was pleased in a way, as he was sure his father would ask difficult questions about what was happening next. Saying goodnight, he made his way to bed. He spent half the night thinking of what path to take. Bright and early the next morning, his mother woke him with a cup of tea.

'Your breakfast is ready. You'd better get down stairs before your dad eats it all.'

Arriving at the kitchen table, he sat down next to his father. There was a plate of eggs and bacon waiting for him. This was his last morning at home; later that day he would have to return to the barracks.

Jimmy's father got to his feet. 'Well, since you don't need a lift to town, I have to get going. I've snares to check. It's been great to have you home; try and get back when you can.'

Point the Finger of Blame

Lowering his voice so his wife couldn't overhear, Brian said: 'I know you haven't been telling your ma and me all of what you've been up to, but I trust you lad. So, whatever it is they've asked you to do, think carefully. You've got a good head on your shoulders, but look after yourself lad.'

With that, he shook his son's hand, collected his packed lunch and kissed his wife as he left. Jimmy wasn't surprised at his father's leaving comment; he was only surprised he hadn't questioned him.

Jimmy went back upstairs. He washed, shaved and then collected his bags that he'd packed the night before, checking to make certain he had packed everything. He went back down to the kitchen. His mother was waiting; she had packed him some sandwiches for the journey. Jimmy could see the beginnings of tears in her eyes as she held out her arms and hugged him.

'Take care, son.'

He knew she was thinking of the problems in Korea and of the possibility of fighting.

'Why can't there be peace in the world? What point is there in training lads to kill each other? We're supposed to be civilised.'

Jimmy gave his best reassuring smile and gave her another hug.

With that, he heard the staff car arrive. Pulling himself away, he said goodbye to his mother and walked out to the car. As the car went down the road, he looked back and waved but couldn't see his mother. He was certain she would be looking out of the window. Jimmy took a deep breath and tried to settle his emotions before turning to the driver and introducing himself.

CHAPTER SEVEN

By the time Jimmy arrived back at camp, he'd made up his mind on the path his life would take. As soon as he stepped from the car he was approached by one of the sergeants and told to report to the C.O's office early the next morning. The rest of the lads greeted him with questions. They wanted to know how he had swung so much leave after a spell in the kitchens. He jokingly told them it was because he was the best spud basher and washer upper the army had ever seen.

Getting up the next morning, Jimmy made certain he was as smart as he could be before reporting to the office as ordered. On his arrival, Captain McGee greeting him with a salute which Jimmy returned.

'Stand at ease McLeod; I hope you have given consideration to the matter we discussed.'

'Yes sir. I would like to volunteer for sniper training.'

'Right, I'll get the ball rolling straight away; no point in wasting time. You'll be sent to receive special training as soon as it can be arranged.'

With that, he picked up the phone and contacted H.Q. Putting down the phone after a brief conversation, he turned back to Jimmy.

'McLeod, it seems there is a new intake starting tomorrow, so you will be taken to the training camp at eleven-hundred hours today. Bring all of your kit and personal belongings and make certain you leave nothing behind. The rest of the men have already left for the firing ranges so you won't be seeing them again, but don't leave any personal messages. We will come up with a cover story.'

Jimmy was a bit surprised at the speed things were moving and was soon back at the billet packing all his things. It didn't take him long as didn't have that much to take. He checked over his locker and bed space once more. He was glad he didn't have to worry about questions from the other lads. Sitting on the striped bunk he contemplated the future. Jimmy hoped he had made the right decision; he would have liked to talk it over with someone and had expected the commander to have said more but, as his father would've said, he'd made his bed now, he would have to lie in it. Looking around the room where he'd had so much fun with his new friends, he regretted not being able to leave them a message to say goodbye; but, with an explicit order not to, he picked up his bags and headed to the main offices where he was to be collected.

Jimmy was soon sitting in a jeep, heading deeper into the countryside. After about three quarters of an hour, they turned off down a one-track road into another glen. After another three miles there was a barrier across the road; the jeep's driver was greeted by an armed soldier who demanded to see both their passes. The driver showed his pass and Jimmy got his out of his top pocket and showed it to the soldier. Then the barrier was lifted to let them through. Once through the

Point the Finger of Blame

barrier, they turned left on to a dirt track. Jimmy could just make out some huts and tents about half a mile ahead. The site was at the base of a mountain and tucked in among some trees. It was clear to Jimmy that the only way anyone could spot the camp was if they were going along the track. The terrain was much the same as his home, a mixture of woodland and open heath with a glorious backdrop of mountains. Just as they arrived the rain started to pour down. The jeep was met by a burly sergeant.

'A new recruit for you, Sarge,' said the driver with a knowing smirk.

These were the first words the driver had spoken throughout the drive. On leaving the camp, Jimmy had tried to make conversation with the driver but soon gave up, realising that he would get nowhere.

Jimmy jumped out of the jeep and started to go to the back to get his bags.

'Where are you going?' shouted the sergeant.

'Fetching my bags, Sir,' replied Jimmy.

He quickly realised he should have stood to attention and saluted first but in his rush to get out of the heavy rain he had forgotten. Turning, he stood to attention and awaited the expected rebuke.

'Right lad, twenty press-ups. Now.'

On rising up from the final press up, he felt the sergeant's foot in the centre of his back and he was pushed face down in the mud. The sergeant bent down and shouted in Jimmy's ear.

'Get this into your thick skull; you don't even piss unless I tell you to.'

Lying with his face in the mud, Jimmy was doing his best to control his temper. The sergeant let him stand up and looked Jimmy straight in the eye.

'What's your name?'

Jimmy tried to keep his voice neutral. 'McLeod, sir.'

He couldn't keep all the venom out of his voice.

Continuing to look Jimmy straight in the eye, the sergeant shouted once more: 'You'd like to hit me, wouldn't you McLeod? Well go on, try it, you have my permission in front of a witness.'

Needing no more encouragement, Jimmy exploded, throwing a hefty punch. The next thing he knew, he was back in the mud looking up at the sergeant who was sneering down at him.

'You have thirty minutes to clean yourself up, and then I will give you a full kit inspection. Your hut is number four. Make sure you're ready in time.'

With that, the sergeant turned and marched away. Jimmy could hear the driver laughing as he drove off.

Jimmy picked up his bags from the mud where the driver had thrown them and headed for the hut. His temper was not improved by the fact that he had been hit into the mud but, at least due to the rain, he didn't think his humiliation had been witnessed by anyone but the driver. Thankfully, the hut was empty when he got there. Jimmy had a quick look around the hut; there was a small wardrobe and a stool, with a mirror on the wall by each bunk. On the end wall, a Union Flag was tacked up. The floors were boarded out but there was no heating. Jimmy headed straight for a bunk that was not made up and, after checking the wardrobe was empty, he started to try and clean up his kit. Gradually, his temper cooled and he realised what an idiot he had

Point the Finger of Blame

been. It was obvious that the sergeant had known he could have easily stopped Jimmy or he wouldn't have made the challenge. It was dead on half an hour when the sergeant entered the hut. Jimmy quickly stood to attention and looked straight ahead. He had changed into his combats as his uniform was still plastered in mud despite his best efforts; but, he'd folded it correctly and at least he had cleaned himself up and made sure his boots shone. The sergeant eyed him from head to toe and looked at the folded clothes on the bunk.

'Not a bad effort, McLeod, but your uniform's a disgrace. So is the hut.'

He was rubbing his finger along the top of the door.

'There's a wash-house next to hut number seven. Get your uniform clean, and then report to me in the command tent.' With that, he turned and walked out.

Picking up his uniform, he headed to hut number seven and went into the washroom. He washed his uniform in the shower and looked around for somewhere to dry it out.

'Hut eight,' a voice bellowed out.

He looked around but couldn't see anyone. Picking up his uniform, he headed toward hut eight. This turned out to be a drying room. Hanging his uniform to dry he quickly returned to the wash-house and had a quick shower and hair wash before reporting to the command tent, wondering all the time what he had let himself in for.

Jimmy was pleased to see that at least the rain had stopped. As he approached the command tent, he could see the sergeant waiting for him. He quickly stood to attention and saluted.

'Stand at ease, McLeod; I had good reports of you but you've not given me a good impression so far. Let's see what you're made of. Follow me.'

He turned and walked to the back of the tent.

Pointing up at the mountain, he said: 'See that yellow flag? That's a round trip of about three miles. It's the steepest part of the mountain so I'll give you a time of thirty minutes; with a pack on your back, you could be the first ever to do it. If not, there are some latrines that need cleaning. On with the pack son, your time starts now.'

Jimmy quickly put on the pack and set off. He set himself a steady pace; he was used to climbing mountains. He used to race with his friends at home and knew the best way to pace himself. The pack was taking a toll on him; carrying such a heavy object was not his normal practice when racing up a mountain side. By the time he reached the flag his calves and shoulders were aching. He looked at his watch; it had taken him seventeen minutes to get to the yellow flag. Going downhill would be easier but he knew, if he pushed too fast, he risked falling. He set off once more, pacing himself carefully. As he reached the command tent he glanced at his watch: ten seconds to spare.

The sergeant had watched his progress and was impressed.

'Well done lad, you nearly beat my time. While you were up there, did you spot anything?'

'Yes sir. There were three men hiding in the heather in separate places.'

'Point them out.'

Point the Finger of Blame

'There's one on the left, fifty yards from the flag; one twenty yards higher than the flag; the last one's a hundred yards up the mountain.'

'Very good, but you missed the one fifteen yards back from the washroom.'

Jimmy could see that he had gained some respect from the sergeant for his observational skills. He instinctively knew that the sergeant would never give such praise unless it was tempered with a 'could do better' comment on the end.

'Right lad, I think you've earned yourself a meal and a cuppa. Go over to the canteen, they're still serving up. I'll get the other lads off the mountain.'

Jimmy didn't wait to be told twice. He took his pack back to his bunk and headed over to the canteen. His altercation with the sergeant on his arrival was soon proved to be false as he sat down with his meal. It wasn't long before he was having his leg pulled by the other soldiers present. But, at least it appeared he had easily beaten the other lads in his recent trip up the mountain.

Jimmy soon settled in and made friends amongst the other lads. They were all there for sniper training, so for the first time Jimmy was able to talk freely about the decision he had made. It seemed most of the lads had the same concerns as him when it came to killing in cold blood. It gave them all a common bond and they worked well together, despite being a very competitive group.

The next month was taken up with nonstop training in survival techniques, unarmed combat, orienteering and rifle practice. After a week, Jimmy and the other members of the group were taken out into the forest, dropped off a short distance apart and left for half an hour before the tracker dogs were sent out on their trail. After the drop off, Jimmy moved away and started to cover his tracks. But he knew he needed to cover his smell if he was to shake off the tracker dogs. Jimmy soon found a rotting rabbit carcass; he quickly rubbed the body over his clothes, face and hands. Then, putting the carcass on the ground, he scuffed his boots in the remains. He had often watched his father's dogs rolling in carcasses to hide their scent and thought if it worked for them it should work for him. Quickly moving a short distance away, he hid himself in the taller heather and, lying flat and still, he waited for the tracker dogs to arrive. He could hear them approaching and knew that this had been his best chance of evading them. He heard the sergeant's voice as the group found one after another of the hiding group. It was getting dark and Jimmy had managed to avoid detection for several hours. The dogs had found his original trail but, as he had hoped, hadn't been able to follow him from the point where he found the dead rabbit. Jimmy was beginning to get cramp from staying still but managed not to move or make a noise.

He heard the sergeant call out for him to show himself as he had passed the test. Not quite sure if this was a trick, he decided to take the risk and expose his position, as he knew it was several hours since the previous person had been found. Instead of just standing up, he crept down to the land-rover before letting anyone spot him.

The sergeant grinned and said 'well done lad'; he then caught the odour from Jimmy.

Point the Finger of Blame

'What the... have you rolled in fox's shit or something?'

'Must have done Sarge,' he replied, not wanting to give away his secret.

The other lads weren't that happy at sharing the back of the land-rover back to base and were only too keen for him to use the shower first when they returned. Despite this, his hut mates said they could smell him all night and threatened to make him sleep outside. Jimmy did very well in the course, not only staying undetected by the tracking team but achieving best shot and survival; only being beaten to second place in the unarmed combat section.

The sergeant was pleased that none of the lads dropped out. After passing the course, all the men were promoted to corporal which came as a surprise to most of them. To celebrate, the sergeant took them all to the nearest pub to celebrate. To their surprise, he said all the drinks were on him. Jimmy had never been a heavy drinker but drank a couple of pints and relaxed for the first time in weeks. There was a great deal of singing and then someone started up a darts match. The sergeant sat next to Jimmy and turned toward him.

'Jimmy, you're the best lad through the training so far. In fact, the best I've ever seen. The war in Korea is about to hit up and without doubt you'll be sent out. Keep your wits about you and do as you have in training and you'll make it back okay. When you do get back, look me up son. Remember, don't waste any shots, only fire when you're sure and never forget the enemy will be after you the minute you shoot; when you do go into the base, report any unusual activity, no matter how small.'

DEREK SMITH

With that, he stood up, as if embarrassed by opening up to Jimmy. He went to play darts with the other men.

At closing time, the sergeant called the men together and drove them back to base. Although they all had a great time, none of the men were drunk. It was as if they had suspected another test. On the way back, they all started to sing and continued until lights out.

The next morning, they were told that the war with Korea had started and that they would all be assigned to different units before setting sail. Jimmy was told to report to the commanding officer's office at ten hundred hours. When he arrived, he found Captain McGee was sitting behind a desk with two United Nations officers; one Canadian and the other American. Jimmy stood to attention and saluted.

'Sit down McLeod. I'll waste no time; both of these men are looking for a sniper to be attached to their forces. You do have some choice in what force you're posted with, as neither is a UK battalion, so you can ask each one any questions you may have.'

Jimmy was surprised to think he would have any say in the matter and somewhat disappointed he wouldn't be attached to a Scottish regiment. Quickly giving the matter some thought he looked at the American officer and asked what, in his mind, was the only real important question he could think of.

'Do you use 303mm rifles Sir?'

'Nope, we don't. We use MIC or MID Garlands, they're .30 calibre.'

Turning to look at the Canadian, Jimmy asked the same question.

'We sure do son, we use the Lee Enfield Mark 4.'

Point the Finger of Blame

Looking back at Captain McGee, he said: 'I don't need to ask anything else, Sir. I'd like to be posted with the Canadian force.'

The three officers were surprised at how quickly Jimmy had made up his mind and the fact that he had only asked the one question. Captain McGee looked at the two officers and back to Jimmy.

'Well, it looks like the decisions made. Report to the camp gate at 0 seven hundred tomorrow and you will be taken to your new base. Good luck.'

'Glad to have you on board, Corporal McLeod,' said the Canadian officer. 'It shows you've got good taste.'

Jimmy smiled and heard the American mutter: 'The lad doesn't know what he's let himself in for with you lot.'

With that, Jimmy saluted and left the office. He hoped he had made the right choice but, at the same time, either way he would be in Korea soon, fighting a war on foreign soil. It all seemed a bit unreal to him after all until his call up papers arrived; he had never travelled more than twenty miles from his home before.

CHAPTER EIGHT

The next morning at six o'clock, Jimmy packed his bags yet again and reported to the main gate. He was soon picked up by a Canadian army jeep. He was the only passenger, so he sat up with the driver. It seemed the officer was flying back to his base rather than driving back with the men. The two young men had soon swapped names and Jimmy asked Doug, the driver, where they were headed. He was surprised to hear that they were headed for southern England. Jimmy had never been out of the highlands and couldn't help but wish he'd had the chance to say goodbye to his parents. He hoped he would be allowed to write to them before he left for Korea. It was a long journey and it gave the young Scot the chance to talk to the Canadian. He found him a likable character, about his own age. As they talked, Jimmy was amazed at the stories Doug told of his home country. Jimmy found it hard to visualise such a large place; he thought the space he'd grown up in was large, but it must have seemed small to the Canadian.

As they passed through the countryside, the landscape became flatter. It wasn't long before Jimmy

Point the Finger of Blame

was missing the mountainous views he was used to and wondering when he would see them next. After a few hours, they passed across the border into England. Jimmy joked that it was his first venture onto foreign soil.

Doug laughed. 'I forgot you Scots used to go to war against the English, didn't you?'

Jimmy smiled. 'Not for a few years now; we sorted that out when we had a Scot on the English throne.'

They carried on driving for several more hours, and then Doug pulled into a small town. They stopped for a quick drink and snack in a small cafe and then set off again. The Canadian was pleased to find that Jimmy had a driver's licence, so they could share the driving. Although this hadn't been authorised, they both felt it would be safer, due to the distances involved. The miles flew by and they stopped again at about three in the afternoon to have a drink and stretch their legs. Even with the pair of them driving, it was still evening by the time they reached Wiltshire. The rolling chalk downs had their own beauty and Jimmy felt there could be lots to explore but doubted he would get the time. He felt more at home when he saw a buzzard soaring on the thermals above the landscape.

On arriving at Bulford Camp, he left his new-found friend and reported to the main office. Before long, he had left his bags in his new billet and reported to the armoury. After introducing himself, the armourer wasted no time in asking why he preferred a 303. It seemed the news of why he had chosen to serve with the Canadians had preceded him.

'Because of the double pressure trigger action of three pounds and five pounds. It gives a much smoother firing action.'

The armourer seemed impressed by Jimmy's answer and took him through to the workshop.

'We need to select your gun and zero the site for you. These guns are specially selected for their accuracy, so look after it well and make sure no one else uses it; don't you use anyone else's gun for that matter.'

After sorting through some of the guns and picking out one, the armourer started to head out the door.

'Grab those boxes of ammo lad,' he said, pointing to some boxes on a shelf.

'Follow me; let's get you out to do some shooting.'

Six hours and hundreds of bullets later, Jimmy could hit a matchstick at thirty yards and a tennis ball at five hundred yards. After that, it was out to the main range where he was soon hitting the bull at eight hundred yards.

'Brilliant shooting,' shouted the armourer.

'But remember, these targets don't shoot back; also, it takes a special sort of man to take a life in cold blood. This will be your main role. But, if you can, your actions will save many lives and perhaps shorten the war in the process.'

Jimmy spent the next couple of weeks using his gun in various situations and honing his map reading and other skills. The armourer's words of wisdom kept coming back to Jimmy when he left the camp with a group of Canadians for Plymouth naval docks.

When they arrived, they found themselves in a larger force being put onto a Royal Naval vessel that would take them to South Korea. To start with it was exciting as Jimmy had never been on a ship before; but boredom soon began to take hold. He, like many others, found being confined to such a small space difficult. The sergeants tried to keep them busy and the men spent many hours doing physical activities that kept them fit. Jimmy hated all the press ups and running on the spot but it did help pass the time; yet, in the end, everything they did became monotonous and most of the men spent a great deal of their spare time playing cards for matchsticks. One of the men had soon won most of the matchsticks on board. Jimmy spent as much time as he could up on deck; at least that way he could watch the seabirds as they flew over and the occasional dolphin in the sea from the ship's bow.

The long voyage gave him time to think over what he had committed himself to. He found himself wondering if he really did have the skills that a good sniper needed. It was all very well doing the training but, until he faced the real thing, he wouldn't know for sure. Jimmy knew he was a good shot but shooting a man in cold blood was a different thing. He only wished he had been able to talk it over with his father; but, at the same time, he was glad his mother wasn't aware of what he would be doing. He had managed to send a short note to them before he left but they had been told not to give any details. He had also written a letter that would be given to them if he didn't make it back. That had really brought home to him exactly what he was heading into. But then, that would have still been the case if he was heading to Korea as an ordinary soldier.

He tried to keep as busy as he could and managed to get hold of some paper and pencils. He spent a long time drawing the birds and other sea life. He found drawing gave him the outlet he needed and allowed him to relax and forget what was happening. The same level of relaxation he had felt as a child watching the wildlife of Scotland. He kept his drawing secret from the friends he'd made but was secretly pleased with how he was progressing. At least his new-found hobby gave him something else to think about and also gave him plenty of practice with his observational skills.

It was a full month later when the ship arrived in the Port at Incheon in South Korea. This was the same port that the very first American force had arrived at, so the locals were used to seeing large naval vessels arriving. The port was a hive of activity and so busy that it looked chaotic to Jimmy's inexperienced eye. There were so many people thronging the dockside, it was hard to work out who was doing what.

Jimmy and the others didn't have time to take in the port as the men were soon disembarked and put into lorries, their kit all piled up in the centre. Although Jimmy was sitting fairly near the back of the lorry, he didn't have much of a view as they sped through the countryside. It was obvious however, that the area had seen action as the vehicles weaved in and out of bomb craters that had damaged the roads. Jimmy thought of the war films he had watched in the past and hoped they weren't attacked by enemy aircraft. Most of the men were silent, lost in their own thought, with the occasional nervous whisper. Jimmy was just turning to his neighbour to speak when the lorry hit a deep pothole and the twenty-odd soldiers in the back of the lorry were thrown about. Some of the men fell on top of kit in the centre of the lorry or onto the men opposite;

much swearing ensued. No damage seemed to have occurred to the lorry and they didn't stop. The men struggled to get back in their seats and put everything back in place as the lorry continued to swerve this way. There was a lot of moaning about the bruises they were all sure they had received in the shakeup, but no one was hurt.

It was nightfall when the convoy arrived at camp, so Jimmy still couldn't get a good look at his surroundings. The men got out of the lorries in silence and stretched their aching and cramped limbs; their names were called out with the hut they had been assigned to and they were told to go straight to their billets. Collecting their kit bags, the men went straight to a series of huts and deposited their belongings on the bunks. Before they had a chance to settle down, the sergeant arrived and told them to head for the mess or they would miss the evening meal. The men didn't need to be told twice and were soon queuing up to collect their supper. There was a nervous tension among the men, very few of them had ventured far from home before joining the forces, although the Canadians had been away from home for some time, having travelled to England before departing once more for Korea. Now, they were in a completely foreign land and facing the prospect of fighting for their lives. None of them seemed to want to talk. After supper, they filed back to the billets and settled down for the night.

The next morning they were woken up at six o'clock, told to have a quick breakfast, and then get ready for parade. They were to be on the parade ground by seven o'clock. Joining the rest of the men in the wash-house, Jimmy had a quick wash; the water was cold but had the effect of waking him up. He went to the mess and joined the queue for breakfast. It was filling but he didn't recognise some of the food on his plate. As soon as he finished, he returned his plate and set off for the parade ground. It was his first real chance to have a look at his surroundings in daylight. The camp was set in a heavily forested area. The clearing stretched away from the camp so that the enemy couldn't creep up on them unseen. Although many of the trees were unfamiliar, he thought the view was similar to that of a heavily wooded wild area in the highlands of Scotland. But what set it apart immediately were the sounds that came from the trees. Jimmy could hear many strange sounding birds and other noises he thought were probably a type of monkey; but he also heard the familiar call of a cock pheasant. Looking up as a flock of birds flew over, he was surprised to see what he thought were starlings but, as they landed, he noticed their pale grey plumage. Turning back to the parade ground, he hoped that any inspection would be quick as his uniform was not at its best. At least the rest of the men looked in a similar state. The men were all relieved that no inspection took place that morning; instead they were told that they would be travelling further into North Korea.

The army had made significant gains of territory and the journey was longer than any of the men imagined. The journey was hard on the men; the roads were little more than dirt tracks full of potholes. They often had to get out and push the lorries out of the deep ruts. The men all ached from trying to keep themselves on the rough seats. The heat became almost unbearable at times and the men all began to get bitten by the many

Point the Finger of Blame

insects. Except for a short break at about midday the convoy kept on the move until that evening, although the progress had often been slow due to the state of what passed for roads. Overnight, the men had the chance to talk to other troops making the return journey; some were injured and others were heading back for a short break at the base camp. What they heard didn't make for pleasant hearing and many of the men became more apprehensive about what lay ahead.

Next morning, they set off once again and the journey repeated itself with the roads getting rougher as they progressed. It was during these overnight stops that the men heard the Chinese army had intervened on the side of the North Koreans, as the United Nations soldiers had pushed their forces to the far north and nearer China. This had added many thousands of enemy troops to the war. The U.N. troops were being pushed back and they were losing much of the territory they had gained in the previous months. The Chinese troops were far more experienced than the North Koreans and more disciplined, as well as being better armed. This meant that the front line was gradually being pushed back, with the allies losing ground daily, and the loss of life on the allied side was increasing. This made the men more apprehensive and what had seemed like a big adventure when they left Great Britain now seemed far grimmer than most had been expecting. Many of the lads had believed the war would soon be over and that the inferior Korean Army would be beaten but, with the Chinese now involved, they knew it would be a far harder task. Jimmy thought he and the other men would be here a long time and didn't relish the task ahead. He knew some of the others had been really excited at the prospect of fighting when they left England but he could see some of those same men had now had second thoughts.

Jimmy and the others soon reached an army base, previously well behind enemy lines, that now seemed not too far from the front line. The sound of fighting could be heard and it had a sobering effect on all the men. The next morning, they had a lecture on keeping within the camp boundaries at all times; the day was to be spent preparing the camp for the monsoon season. Being used to Scottish weather, Jimmy felt that some of the jobs were a bit over the top. Surely the rain wouldn't be that bad. They had some really heavy storms back home; he'd heard about the monsoons and it appeared the storms lasted longer than he was used to, but the precautions to him seemed excessive. That night, the men turned in early, the work that day had been made much harder by the hot and humid weather. Jimmy, like most of the others found it hard to sleep due to the humidity, even though they were exhausted. Some of the old hands fared much better and could be heard snoring, which made it even harder for the others to sleep.

The next morning the new men, including Jimmy, were assigned to their platoons to fill spaces left by the fighting; the army had suffered some heavy losses. Once assigned, the men were briefed on their mission. Jimmy's section was to take a nearby hill and hold it against the enemy. Whoever held the hill had the advantage over the supply route which was vital to the retreating soldiers. After the men left to join their sections, he was taken to see the captain, who explained that Jimmy's job was to find the location of

Point the Finger of Blame

the enemy and, if safe to do so, take out any high ranking enemy officers and report back on enemy positions. The captain asked if he was familiar with the equipment and ensured that he could send the Morse code messages back to base. He was also given a personal code to memorise so that he would be able to identify himself to the various messengers, who would contact him and the local army commanders should he need to report in directly.

Later that day, the troop set off to the base of the hill. The fighting was hard but, despite some loss of men, it took the Canadians only two days to drive the enemy back and take possession of the hill. They saw no sign of the Chinese during the fighting. The North Koreans seemed poorly equipped and no match for their tough opponents. The more seasoned troops warned the newcomers that it wasn't always the case and not to underestimate the hard fighting ahead. They were soon proved right when, just after the men had dug themselves into their new position, a couple of Chinese planes flew over and gave the men hell, firing as they flew overhead. It wasn't long before the enemy planes were attacked by the U.N. air force and driven off. The casualties would have been far worse if the help had come any later. It was a real eye-opener to Jimmy and the others as to the realities of their new lives.

Jimmy had made a conscious effort to keep himself separate from the others, moving frequently among the others so that he wouldn't be missed, as he had been ordered to move out behind enemy lines when darkness fell. He was so successful that only the captain and his sergeant where aware of him leaving the newly set up base. After moving away from the camp, Jimmy spent some time just sitting and listening to the night time sounds. They would be his best ally; he needed to understand the normal night pattern around him. The creatures of the forest would help him pinpoint enemy activity, as their calls would tell him when others were about. However, he knew that any enemy present would also be listening to those same sounds and would have the advantage until he knew all the sounds around him. He saw a type of owl he couldn't recognise hunting over the open area and a small group of deer at the forest edge. It seemed the wildlife were still able to go about their daily business despite the war raging around them.

Over the next few days, Jimmy got to know the forest around him, gradually increasing his knowledge of the area and its inhabitants. After a while, he came across a small camp of the enemy; he was studying their actions when all of a sudden they all made for the cover of their tents, taking their possessions with them. Looking around, he couldn't see the cause of the sudden movement, but he soon found out as the skies darkened and a monsoon storm started. Jimmy found he had been wrong; the monsoon rains were nothing like the storms he was used to in Scotland. It was as if someone was pouring buckets of water over his head. The rain poured down the hillside in torrents, then suddenly, after what seemed like hours, it stopped as quickly as it had arrived. It left Jimmy soaked through to the skin and, more importantly, all his equipment was also soaked through. He had tried to find shelter but in the end had to make do crouching under a large tree to try to keep out the worst of the driving force of the rain.

Point the Finger of Blame

After the downpour stopped, he withdrew some way to inspect his kit and to try to wring out his clothes. He didn't intend to make the same mistake again; luckily, the electronics of his Morse code transmitter came in a waterproof bag, so that was in good order. Carefully checking his gun, he was happy he could fire it safely if needed. He could hear the enemy soldiers as they came out from the shelter of their tents. Moving quietly, he moved back to his previous position overlooking the camp.

Looking around, Jimmy was somewhat surprised to see a general sat outside one of the tents. He hadn't expected to find such a high ranking officer with such a small company. He settled down in a good firing position, resting his gun on his backpack for support, and carefully took the general in his gun sites. With his finger on the trigger, he found himself shaking and unable to pull the trigger. Jimmy finally had the answer to the question he had often asked himself; he was unable to shoot a human being in cold blood. Crouched down in his hiding place, he continued to shake. He felt a coward. Would he be unable to do the job he had been trained for or was this a normal reaction in facing such a situation for the first time? He lay still and quiet, letting these thoughts go through his mind. Slowly, he calmed down and decided to take another look at the camp. The general was nowhere to be seen. Jimmy continued to watch the camp and came to the conclusion that the general had left, as there were fewer soldiers than before in the area. The highest ranking officer now appeared to be a lieutenant and so, taking a deep breath, Jimmy positioned his gun and took aim once again. Blocking out all thought of what he was about to do, he pulled the trigger. The officer fell to the ground, a bullet between his eyes. Jimmy turned and ran into the forest before the men in the camp realised what had happened. He was glad for the time he had spent learning the area; it allowed him to escape the enemy soldiers as they searched for their officer's killer. Jimmy kept going even when all sound of the searchers faded. In fact, he didn't stop until he reached the Canadian base camp at the top of the captured hill. Managing to get close enough to be clearly seen by the guards, he identified himself and reported to the sergeant.

The sergeant took one look at Jimmy and gestured to him to sit down.

'Here lad. Have a cup of tea and let me know what happened.'

The sergeant guessed that Jimmy had killed his first man. He had seen several new snipers arrive back from their first mission and knew the signs.

Letting Jimmy compose himself, he sat quietly of a moment before saying: 'Did you get one lad?'

Jimmy nodded. He took a deep breath and made his report, trying not to forget any of the details. He felt ashamed of his weakness in not killing the general. Once he had finished, the sergeant nodded.

'I've seen it before, it won't get any easier lad. If it did you'll just become a killing machine. You have a job to do, an important one; try to look on it as such, it's a bit like being a gamekeeper. The difference is your pests here aren't animals, even if they act like 'em.'

Pausing for a short time, he continued: 'Go and write your report and, don't worry, no one will blame you for freezing a bit on your first mission. Once you've written your report, go to the cook, get yourself a good meal and then get your head down for a couple of hours. You leave again once dusk comes. Report here for your orders before you leave.'

With that, Jimmy left to find a quiet spot to write his report; at the same time, he tried to block out the fact that he had taken a life in cold blood. He handed his finished report to the sergeant and headed over to get himself some food. Jimmy had never felt less like eating, but forced the food down. He didn't get the chance of hot food when he was out in the field; he wasn't able to light a fire as the smoke would give his position away. Jimmy went and found himself a quiet place and got his head down for a couple of hours before he was summoned to see the senior officers. They asked him a few questions about his report. Afterwards, he went back and got a few more hours sleep in the relative safety of the camp. He could rest easier knowing he didn't have to worry about being discovered by the enemy. At least when he was in camp, Jimmy didn't have to worry that someone would find him.

Later that evening, after collecting a new set of orders, Jimmy collected up his gear and slipped out of camp. After his talk with the sergeant, he realised that it was to be expected that he should have some qualms about what he was being asked to do. But, he was determined to go ahead and try to make a difference to the war effort, no matter what it took.

CHAPTER NINE

The monsoon season made Jimmy's job harder in many ways, but at least the rain washed his tracks away. He soon learned to spot the warning signs of downpours, so that he at least could try to find shelter and keep his equipment dry. Following the monsoon season, the weather got much colder, but drier; the Scottish weather was colder than any he experienced here, so at least he was used to that. One day, walking through the forest, he heard voices in the distance. Stopping to listen, he quickly concluded that there must be a large group of enemy soldiers ahead. Making use of the thick vegetation, he crept in the direction of the sounds. Carefully concealing himself, he looked toward the enemy camp and saw a mass of activity. There were what appeared to be hundreds of Korean and Chinese soldiers in a clearing. Many of them were well armed with guns, whilst other seemed to have only a very basic kit.

This didn't surprise Jimmy as there never seemed to be enough equipment among the enemy soldiers. What did surprise him was the amount of men gathered in one place. From his observations, he concluded that they were going to try to take the hill back from the Canadians. He turned and carefully moved a couple of miles back from the camp, making sure that the enemy lookouts remained unaware of his presence. Carefully concealing himself, he sent a coded message back to warn his superiors of the numbers of enemy not far from their position on the hill. He estimated that they were less than twenty miles from the front line. The one thing Jimmy had learnt was to always look for anything in any given area that might be useful to him. Just before he had spotted the camp, he had come across some bear droppings; they reminded him at the time of the trick he'd used in training camp. As always, he had made a mental note and stored the information. After sending his message, he collected some of the droppings before going back to the outskirts of the enemy camp. Finding himself a good spot, he settled down to watch the activity in the camp so he would be able to warn the Canadians when they left the clearing.

After a while, he spotted a general with a group of men; it was the same man he'd had in his sights when he froze. Looking round his position for enemy lookouts, he concluded there were none in the immediate vicinity; so, he found a spot where he could rest his gun. Taking careful aim he squeezed the trigger and fired. As soon as the bullet left the gun, he knew he had killed the general. He turned and, making sure he kept under cover of the forest, moved as fast as he could through the undergrowth.

This time, the reaction in the camp was far quicker and he soon heard soldiers coming after him. He also heard dogs with the men. It wouldn't be so easy this time to get away, but Jimmy knew this area and had made mental preparations for just such a getaway, after he had sent his signal.

Once he had covered a short distance, he stopped and covered himself and his kit with the droppings he had collected earlier. They smelt foul and almost made him gag. But, it was a matter of life and death. He was careful not to block the end of his rifle; he might need to try and shoot his way out if the trick failed. Then, he quickly climbed a tree and hid both himself and his kit in the higher branches. It was a good job he travelled light.

The trick worked once again and he stayed undiscovered; about an hour after the enemy had left the area he was hiding in, he carefully looked around to make certain they hadn't posted any lookouts. Once he was sure he was alone, Jimmy climbed down from the tree and made his way back to base as fast as he could. As he neared the base, he spotted several Koreans and Chinese making their way up the hill. They were obviously scouts checking the area. Much as he was tempted to kill them, he resisted the impulse and found a hiding place to send off another signal. He was told to keep an eye out for enemy snipers and be prepared to take cover when the bombardment of the attackers took place.

Jimmy knew of a small cave nearby; the entrance was covered with thick brambles where he could hide, if he could make it there without being seen. His field craft had never been so needed. He was thankful for all his father's lessons of keeping out of sight when stalking the deer at home. Getting to the rocks, he crept into the cave, making sure that he didn't disturb the covering vegetation. To call the space a cave was a bit of an exaggeration as it was barely big enough to hide in, but it was the best place he could think of. It wasn't long before the main attack force arrived. Jimmy was astounded at their numbers; the hill appeared to be covered in the enemy. There were so many, they seemed like ants going up an anthill. He realised that, if he hadn't been able to warn the camp, they would have been quickly overwhelmed. The Canadians soon opened fire with everything they had. Jimmy carefully observed the carnage as the enemy soldiers fell. But no matter how many fell, more seemed to take their place. Jimmy decided it would be better if he completely hid himself, so he got as far as he could into the rocks and kept still and quiet, resisting any further impulse to observe events. If he was spotted, he hated to think what his fate would be. At least by now he had almost got used to the smell of himself covered in the bear droppings.

The battle continued for most of the night and, at times, the Canadians nearly lost possession of the hill; somehow, they managed to hang on to their position. By morning, the firing had stopped and Jimmy looked cautiously out from his hideaway. The hillside was covered in the dead and dying. The smell of blood and gunpowder filled the air. The site shocked Jimmy as the numbers involved were huge. He remembered his mother's comments on wars and how she hadn't been able to understand why they trained young men to be killers. After all, there had already been two world wars; yet, that still wasn't enough killing for anyone. Jimmy wondered what her reaction would be if she could see the amount of death one battle had caused. At that moment, he realised that his job was no different than any other soldiers; they were all trained killers. In fact, he was almost certainly killing less than many of the other soldiers. After watching for a while, he left the cover of the rocks and carefully stretched his aching muscles. Keeping covered, he made his way up the hill. Getting close enough to be seen, he called the password to the Canadians and was let through into the camp. The camp soldiers were disgusted by the smell and made their feelings clear. Jimmy was amazed that the men were worried about something like that when the camp was surrounded by the stench of death. One of the men escorted him to the command tent where he gave a quick report before being told to go and clean himself up, get something to eat, and return afterwards for a full debrief.

It was rare for anyone at the camp to be given so much precious water to wash with, so Jimmy made the most of it. After cleaning his kit, he had a thorough wash and set his clothes out to dry before going to get some food. He knew he still had a slight smell of bear but he felt it was at an acceptable level. He went and got himself some hot food before returning to the command tent. After a debriefing, he helped the others around the camp in getting the wounded settled as they waited to be evacuated before getting some sleep. An uneasy ceasefire was in place as each side collected their injured.

The enemy withdrew for a while as it seemed, with the element of surprise lost, they were unwilling for the moment to lose more men until reinforcements arrived. Both sides had suffered high casualties, both in dead and dying, for such a small piece of land. But it wasn't long before the battle for the hill restarted and, over the next few weeks, the Canadians were forced back by

Point the Finger of Blame

sheer weight of numbers and were once more on the retreat toward the South Korean border.

This continued right along the frontline and, in the next few months, more and more battles were fought over small pieces of land, with the North Koreans and the Chinese gaining ground all the time. Occasionally the NATO forces would push the enemy back, but overall they were getting forced back over territory they had taken in the early days of the war, before the Chinese army had joined in. Jimmy spent most of his time behind enemy lines, finding and reporting on the positions of the enemy. Occasionally he would have the opportunity to target the officers and kill them. Several times he had to hole up to avoid snipers from the other side. On two occasions, he managed to take out Chinese snipers successfully. He gradually found himself becoming hardened to his role and found he no longer relived the killings in his dreams as he had done on earlier occasions.

A couple of months later, Jimmy was sat in his tent writing one of his rare letters home to his parents; this was about the only time now when he did think about what he was doing. He knew his mother wouldn't understand why he had taken the choices he had. But, at the same time, he was fairly certain his father would understand and even approve, knowing that a good sniper could save lives as well as take them.

He was about half way through the letter when a sergeant came and said: 'The C.O. wants to see you corporal.'

'Can I just finish this letter Sarge?' Jimmy asked hopefully.

DEREK SMITH

'No, an order is an order lad, you know that. Get going now.'

Jimmy folded the letter carefully and put it in his pocket before following the sergeant out of the tent. Dragging his feet a little, he trudged through mud that was inches deep. It had been raining heavily for the last three days. Getting to the commanding officer's tent, he stopped, saluted, and called out his name.

'Corporal McLeod reporting, Sir.'

'Come in,' came the C.O's voice from within. 'Take a seat,' he said.

Gesturing to a chair in front of his desk, he didn't even look up. Once Jimmy was sat down, the C.O glanced up.

'We have a little job that needs doing and I think you're just the man for it. The Chinese have moved down from the north, closer to our position. They appear to be rallying at a base camp five miles from here. Our spotter planes have taken photos and it looks like a battalion. If more arrive, their sheer numbers will allow them to overrun our defences. We can't get air cover at the moment as they're busy elsewhere. So, the Yanks are sending a battery of artillery to assist us. I want you to find a place as near as you can to the enemy camp and guide the shells in, as they will be firing from this side of the hill. You'll be given a field telephone. This is a dodgy mission and not your normal task; however, your field craft should enable you to remain hidden and I can think of no one better suited.'

The C.O pushed some photos toward Jimmy and pointed at the enemy positions. He was familiar with the terrain in the area and could immediately see the problem.

Point the Finger of Blame

'To the right on the high ground is an old farmhouse; it's not very big but probably a good place to observe from. The enemy doesn't occupy any of the land between us and the farmhouse, although there is plenty of firing taking place. Leave tonight after dark. First thing in the morning, we open fire; only give the gunners the information they need and be careful not to give your position away in anything you say. Now memorise the map and then get yourself prepared. Good luck McLeod.'

With that, Jimmy took another look at the map, stood up, saluted the commanding officer, turned and left the tent. He always found the meetings with the C.O very one-sided; it was as if he were just a thing to be ordered about with no thought as to what happened to him. Then again, he thought, it must be hard to just keep ordering men into these situations; but, it would be better, to his mind, if the officers could at least look at him when handing out dangerous assignments.

Jimmy went back to his billet, collected what he needed, and then met up with the sergeant, who took him to collect the field telephone.

'Contact us as soon as the first shell lands, using the code name 'Buster'. We will only answer to confirm each time. Good Luck.'

The sergeant gave Jimmy a pat on the back.

Jimmy picked up his gear and set off through the darkness. He knew the area well, but was careful to keep his ears and eyes open; Jimmy was well aware that the enemy had people out all the time and, like him, they knew how to move quietly. Using all his skill and cunning, he made it to the small farmhouse undetected. Checking to make certain there was no one else in the area, he went inside. Carefully checking out all the rooms, he made his way to an upstairs room overlooking the target area. Looking out the window, he could see the enemy's camp fires in the distance. By the glow, he could also see a mass of enemy vehicles, despite the fact that they were hidden in the trees. He wondered how the photos had been taken without detection as they had looked like they had been taken from ground level and not overhead by plane.

Dawn was breaking and it wasn't long before the first allied shell landed. Falling short of the target by some distance, Jimmy radioed the results.

'Buster up 500.'

He continued to guide the barrage right through the camp, scattering the enemy. Some of the lorries started to move away to the right, heading up the hill towards him. He started to guide the shells towards them, but some were landing too close for comfort. He decided that finding a new base was the best idea. Turning toward the door, he was confronted by a Korean standing in the doorway. They faced each other and, at that second, a shell landed right behind the Korean, killing him instantly. Jimmy ran into the undergrowth surrounding the farmhouse. The Koreans were launching a counter attack. Their numbers had been decreased and quite a few of their lorries were destroyed, but there were still enough left to be dangerous; it was plain that they were still up for a fight. Looking around, Jimmy decided that the Korean had been on his own, as there didn't appear to be anyone else in the immediate area. He left the farmhouse, even though he had been told to stay in the area and await

Point the Finger of Blame

further instructions. Jimmy climbed up into one of the trees a couple of hundred yards away and watched.

The Koreans were attacking the allied lines, breaking through in one area and forcing the allies back. The fighting was fierce and the enemy numbers were far greater than they had first thought. The fighting went on for hours and the allies were gradually being forced back. By that afternoon, the allies had lost several miles of ground. Jimmy himself had moved several times to keep his presence unknown, maintaining radio silence. Then, the allies were supported by American fighter planes and a situation of stalemate seemed to be arising, with neither side getting the upper hand. Jimmy continued to keep on the move, following the line back toward the new front. Creeping uphill through the thick undergrowth, he felt the ground give way. He fell into a hole. Checking himself over, he seemed to be unhurt and still had hold of all this kit. Looking around, he was completely hidden by vegetation.

Carefully looking around in the dim light, the hole appeared to be about four foot deep with just a small amount of light coming through the undergrowth above him; he couldn't see the back wall and was unsure if anything else was sharing the hole with him. It was quiet, so he decided to risk climbing out to have a look around. Carefully reaching an opening in the undergrowth, he looked out. Below, he spotted a group of Chinese soldiers about half a mile away. There were several lorries and a jeep; the soldiers were clustered around the jeep. It looked like they were reading a map, spread out on the bonnet. Jimmy couldn't resist it. Carefully placing his rucksack on the rim of the hole, he rested his gun, took careful aim, and shot the officer in the head before diving back into the hole. Once the undergrowth had settled back down, Jimmy listened carefully. He thought he heard something else in the hole with him, then it stopped.

He cursed himself. That had been a stupid thing to do. The enemy hadn't known he was on the hill and they would now be looking for him. He was sure he had killed the officer, but that would be little consolation if he were discovered. Jimmy knew he would have the enemy soldiers looking for him and to make matters worse, someone, or something was in the hole with him. He could clearly hear something moving at the other end of the hole and he had no option but to stay put and hope that whatever it was wouldn't be as dangerous as the enemy. He tried to stop his mind wondering to the tales he had heard about; the treatment of captured soldiers and how they were tortured by being beaten with rifle butts and having fingernails torn out. He knew that, as a sniper, he wouldn't be treated well. For a while he could hear the enemy searching the area, but it gradually became quiet. Despite his thoughts, he gradually dozed off into an exhausted sleep.

Jimmy woke just after dark. He carefully listened before peering out into the surrounding area; hearing and seeing nothing he crept out of the hole and walked a little way away. Stopping to look and listen once more, he heard a rustle from the direction of the hole. He couldn't believe his eyes as the other occupant walked past a short distance away. He had been sharing his hideout with one of the largest moon bears he had ever seen. The animal was over three foot tall

Point the Finger of Blame

and nearly six foot from head to tail. Jimmy knew that the bears were carnivorous, but they rarely attacked humans; eating mainly small mammals. Nevertheless he still felt a shiver go down his spine. To be in a bear's den and not be attacked was unbelievable; he decided there and then never to mention it to anyone, as he knew he would never be believed. The Koreans believed that the moon bear brought humans great happiness and he was certainly happy not to have been attacked.

Jimmy set off toward the allied lines, carefully avoiding both the Korean and Chinese soldiers. Once into no-man's land, he also had to avoid getting shot by his own side. He carefully made his way through the allied front line and into the base camp. Jimmy walked into the camp just as the sun was rising. The first person he saw was the same sergeant who had taken him to the commanding officer before he had set off. It soon became obvious to Jimmy that the allies had suffered heavy losses in the attack.

'It would have been far worse if you hadn't sent those coordinates. We managed to hit them hard before they got the range on our lads. Thought we'd lost you lad. You'd better come with me and report to the C.O. Then you can get yourself cleaned up and fed.'

The camp was still under fire and the C.O was in a bunker at the rear of the camp. Jimmy gave a full report to the officers, answering as fully as he could. Afterwards, Jimmy was surprised when he was given a week's leave. It was the last thing he had expected, even though he hadn't had any leave since arriving in Korea. He was ready to make the most of the chance. The C.O went on to explain that they wouldn't need his services whilst they regrouped their forces but, once he was back, he would be sent straight out again.

'Make sure you get some rest in amongst the recreation, you will need it.'

With that, Jimmy went and had a cleanup, grabbed a very quick meal and then collected some of his back pay; he headed to the pick-up point for a lorry that was leaving for a small town fifty miles behind the front line. There were about twenty men sat in the back of the lorry and it wasn't long before they were all singing. It always amazed Jimmy how quickly this happened. It seemed, whenever a group of soldiers were together away from the front, someone would start singing and everyone soon joined in. He didn't suppose they would make a choir but, no matter how bad the voice, no one kept silent for long. In between songs, the men would talk about their experiences and wonder how much longer before they could go home.

Once they arrived at the town, Jimmy and his Canadian friends were dropped off at the town centre and given strict instructions on the places and areas of the town where they were permitted. They were told that the truck would pick them up at nine am in the same place in one week's time. The men went straight to the hotel they had been booked into and then headed to the nearest bar; it wasn't long before they were all having a good time. The town was swarming with troops from all the nations of the allied forces, as well as some of the native South Korean soldiers. The brothels were kept busy, as were the escort girls in the bars and clubs; the occasional scuffle broke out, but on the whole no harm was done. The town was used to the soldiers. The locals benefited from the trade, but were

Point the Finger of Blame

also grateful for the help the allies were giving their country.

Jimmy was amazed at one incident; the American red caps arrived and broke up a fight between American troops. They waded in, whistles blowing to stop the fight with batons flying; he couldn't believe how brutal they were. One man was knocked clean out after being hit over the head with one of the batons. About eight soldiers were bundled into the back of the van and taken away. He was glad he hadn't decided on joining the Americans if *that* was how they got treated. But then, he supposed the red caps had been outnumbered and many of the soldiers were drunk. Jimmy also realised that he hadn't seen any other trouble so, for all he knew, all of the military police might be just as bad. He wasn't a heavy drinker, so he thought he had a good chance to stay out of trouble.

By the fourth night, Jimmy had spent most of his money on girls and drink. He was sat with some of his new mates, who were all nearly broke. They were talking about their experiences with one of the men, who admitted he wasn't sure if he had actually killed anyone. His mate argued that he must have done, considering the amount of enemy that had been killed. The argument went back and forth, with the first soldier saying that if you are shooting into so many enemies along with everyone else, who knew who was shot? Jimmy kept quiet; he knew how many people he had killed and didn't what to think about it too much. One of the other snipers he had met up with had notches in his gun, but that wasn't his style. Jimmy preferred not to think too hard about it. After a while, the conversation changed to girls and the atmosphere lightened.

DEREK SMITH

Opposite Jimmy were a group of British soldiers, one of whom was of Jamaican origin; they were all drinking quite heavily and had several of the club's escort girls with them. At about ten o'clock a group of American G.I's came into the club, just as some of the British soldiers were standing up and starting to dance with the escort girls. One of the G.I's took exception to the coloured Brit dancing with a white girl. Jimmy had noticed previously the level of colour prejudice with the American soldiers. It was the first time he had come across colour prejudice in any form. In fact, before he had left Scotland, he had never even met a coloured person.

The G.I walked over and pulled the man away saying: 'That's my girl, nigger.'

With that, a fight broke out between the Brits and the Americans. The G.I suddenly pulled out a knife and stabbed the Jamaican, who fell to the floor. One of his mates checked him and said he was dead; with that, the fight took a more serious turn and spread to others in the bar. Within minutes the red caps entered the bar; they must have been outside when the fuss started. As the men ran out, they were captured by the red caps and bundled into the waiting vans regardless of who they were attached to.

Jimmy decided to try to avoid capture and, in the mayhem, managed to slip out of the building via a toilet window, dropping into the street behind. As he landed, he was spotted by a red cap waiting in the street. Jimmy ran though the streets with the red cap close on his heels. He soon found himself in a part of the town that was out of bounds for the soldiers, but by then he'd lost the red cap.

Point the Finger of Blame

Getting back his breath, Jimmy saw a bar across the street. He went in, ordered a drink and sat at the bar, waiting for things to quieten down before he made his way back to his hotel. He couldn't believe what had happened; it was bad enough being killed by the enemy but to be killed by your own side when you were out having fun made no sense. Glancing round, he saw he was the only soldier in the room; not surprising as it was way off the town centre. There was an abundance of pretty girls and it wasn't long before one of them came to join him. She had long legs and wasn't afraid of showing them off. He bought her a drink out of his dwindling funds. The locals were watching him closely; unable to speak English she was still able to communicate enough for him to know that she wanted him to follow her up to one of the rooms. Jimmy was happy to oblige. He enjoyed female company so stood up and, pretending to be tipsy, staggered slightly as he followed her upstairs into a room with a large double bed. Hanging on the bedstead was a large whip and handcuffs. Jimmy was surprised to see such items but soon put them from his thoughts as the girl sat on the bed and gestured for him to join her. He sat down and began to fondle her; he reached to remove her underwear only to discover that she was a man. Shocked, Jimmy didn't know what to do for a second. He had never come across such a thing before, having never heard of transvestites. To give himself time to think, he pretended to pass out as if blind drunk. Lying there, he felt his pockets being searched one by one. Not having much to lose, Jimmy decided it would be worth losing his remaining funds if it got him out of the situation.

After all his money had been taken, Jimmy heard the man leaving the room. Jimmy lay still for a while, wondering just what he had got himself into. Opening his eyes slowly, he looked around in the semi-darkness to make sure he was alone, before sitting up. He sat on the edge of the bed for several minutes, collecting his thoughts and wondering what to do next. Deciding he had stayed there long enough, he got up and made his way to the window, concluding that it might be the best way out. But he was unable to open it, nor could he see an easy way down to the ground if he forced it. Instead, he went toward the door and, opening it, he made his way down the stairs, across the bar, and outside. He did not look at any of the occupants; he could hear them sniggering but there was nothing he could do as he was outnumbered. Jimmy quickly retraced his steps back to the area of town he started his evening in and then walked back to the hotel. He thought he'd had a lucky escape, even if it had cost him all his remaining money.

The last two days of his leave were spent playing cards for matches with the other guys who had spent out. He never told a soul what had happened as he felt such a fool. His experience in town had made him wonder just what humans were capable of. First the stabbing of the Jamaican lad and the way the red coats had treated their own side, together with what had happened to him later, made him realise just how cheap a human life could be. After all, they were in Korea as part of a force to help the locals, yet they were willing to rob the very people who were laying down their lives for them. Thinking about it, he felt that his job as a sniper fitted into the mould. Why should he think anymore of

Point the Finger of Blame

killing a man than a rabbit on the estate? Men, after all, became worse than animals given the chance. He vowed from that day on that he would no longer worry about his role in the war, but just get through it and get back home.

Each time he killed, he found it easier. Jimmy became one of the most feared snipers and killed many high-ranking enemy officers as well as several enemy snipers. His commanders told him that his actions were helping to shorten the war and he received several commendations for his actions, as well as a promotion to sergeant. Although this would not have happened had he been an ordinary soldier, quite a few of the snipers carried that rank even with short terms of service. The promotion made no real difference to Jimmy as he wasn't in the position to have men serving under him, but it did mean he could send his parents extra money home. But, on receiving news of his promotion, he did wonder what the lads he had been in basic training with would think of him now that he was one of the dreaded sergeants. Jimmy didn't know the number of men he had killed, it had become just a job to him. He hadn't even noticed how hardened to killing he had become. He no longer had any qualms about his role, but instead looked on it as what he did best.

It was mid-winter of 1952; it was cold and looked like snow was on the way. The fighting continued, first with one side gaining ground and then the other, with many casualties on both sides. The men were becoming disillusioned as they had all thought that, with the might of America on their side, the war would have been over by now. But the enemy was much tougher than first thought, with the added advantage of being on their own soil. The Koreans' supply chain came overland from China, but the allies had to contend with a sea journey. There was a steady flow of both supplies and men coming over the Chinese border, which the allies hadn't been able to slow. As the winter weather worsened and snow fell deep on the ground, Jimmy and the other snipers found their missions slowing. The tracks they created in the snow made every mission more difficult and discovery inevitable.

Jimmy did most of his work from the trenches, when he could fire across the lines at the enemy officers. He had heard that sometimes the enemy would fool the snipers by getting private soldiers to wear officer's uniforms. He had no way of knowing if this was true, so pushed the thought to the back of his mind; after all, an enemy was an enemy. By careful observation, he and the other snipers could often tell who was who by the actions of their targets. As with the NATO army, the officers had a certain air about them. The higher the rank, the farther behind the front line the officers could be found. Sometimes, Jimmy shot to injure instead of kill. He figured that if his shot injured a target, he would be sent home from the front line and the result would be the same. He knew the idea was to intimidate the officers by making them feel like they were targets but he figured a few less deaths couldn't make that much difference. As Jimmy was in the camps more, it gave him extra opportunities to write home and receive his post. He had never been a great letter-writer and he wasn't able to say much, but at least he figured it would make his mother feel better to at least know he was still alive.

Point the Finger of Blame

Come spring, Jimmy was called to go to headquarters; when he got there, he noticed that there was a lot of the top brass around. He couldn't help but think something big must be going on. Entering an office he had been told to report to, he joined several others. They all sat down in some chairs which were set out before a desk. After a few moments, an American general entered and stood behind the table, facing the men.

'Right men, I won't waste any time. You are here today because you have been selected for your war records to date. You are the six top snipers in the field at this time. We have a mission for you.'

The men looked at each other with interest. The same thought ran though all the men's minds. What mission would need six snipers?

'Your mission is to find the enemy's main supply routes and pinpoint them for the air force. They have been using mules through the forest for much of the stuff they are bringing in and the planes are having trouble finding them. You will be dropped in behind enemy lines but, after you have completed your mission, you will need to find your own way out.'

With this, the General paused.

'You will each take a carrier pigeon with you which you will use to send back the map references once you have them. You will each be dropped in different areas by helicopter at night.'

This sounded risky to Jimmy but he could see that it would be too far to walk in.

'Any questions?' The General's voice penetrated Jimmy thoughts.

'Yes Sir,' said Jimmy. 'How do you know where to drop each of us?'

The General grinned.

'It's a dense forest, so we are going to drop each of you off in a different area; these areas, our intelligence has suggested, will be in the general area of one of these routes, but hopefully not too close. There should be no need for soldiers to be in the areas we are dropping you, as it's a long way behind the enemy's front line. By dropping you off separately, we hope to have a better chance of one of you finding what we are looking for.'

Pausing for a moment to see if anyone had any questions, he continued.

'We are limiting the risk by using the pigeons; they were used with great success in World War Two and mean you can remain in complete radio silence. Well, since that is it, I will let you go and get some practice dropping from a helicopter. You will be given maps just before you leave and have the opportunity to ask further questions. Good luck lads.'

With that, the General gave a salute, turned, and left the room.

After he had gone, the men all looked at each other in amazement. Then they started to going over what they had been told. It seemed to them that most, if not all of them, were not expected to get back after the mission. It was a chilling thought. After a few minutes, they were collected and taken to the training ground to practice their helicopter descent. It seemed they weren't going to be parachuted in but instead lowered into the forest. Due to the terrain, it was felt the only way to get them in. A parachute would just get caught up in the trees and make landing dangerous. Also, it would need to be pulled out of the trees to prevent the enemy knowing what was happening.

They were to be flown to the area and then lowered on a T-bar into the forest below. When they discussed this with the pilot, he said it would be the only way as there were very few clearings where the helicopter could land. The men all went up in the helicopter and then it would hover just above the height of the trees. The men would then hold on to a metal T-bar and sit on the edge of the open door, before pushing themselves out. The men found it tough to hold on as they were lowered down. They had to get used to the swing and imagine what it would be like being lowered amongst the trees, as well as in the pitch dark. They would have to carry all their kit, including their pigeons, down with them. The instructor warned that they would have to let go before their feet touched the ground, to avoid electrocution as the chopper generated static and they would act as an earth if they didn't. They practiced again and again until their arms felt like they would drop off.

The men were to take off that evening, so spent the afternoon trying to get some rest. They were all apprehensive about the drop off, but they knew it had to be done. All of the men had been in difficult positions more than once, so they weren't overly worried about the mission once they had successfully landed. Each of the men had learnt to live with the danger of being on their own in the jungle, with the enemy around them, and coped with the pressure in their own way.

Later that evening, they went and collected their kit and pigeons before heading off to the helicopter. The flight into the jungle was fast and low, trying to avoid the enemy from knowing just how far behind the front line they were travelling. The men sat in total silence, each preparing mentally for the challenge ahead. Once they reached the drop off zone, the pilot assessed the situation and selected the spot he was to drop the first sniper. Jimmy was to be the first one to go. He went toward the door of the helicopter and waited until it opened. Then, sitting at the entrance, he gripped the T-bar above his head. It was almost pitch black and he hoped the pilot had picked a good spot. He pushed out of the door and immediately started to be lowered. He was worried the updraft would draw him up into the rotors; but, this had all been sorted and he was slowly lowered down. He peered into the darkness, trying to gauge the distance to the ground and, when he thought he could see it coming towards him, he let go.

He had misjudged and was higher than anticipated, so fell right into the middle of a bush. He was hurt but, other than a few bruises he was sure he would have in the morning, okay. The helicopter was soon out of both sight and hearing. Once he had got his wind back, he headed into the forest, judging his bearings from the stars. He stopped by a large tree and, taking his rucksack off his back, quickly checked his gun; he also fed and watered his pigeon before settling down with this back to the tree. Unbelievably, he was soon asleep.

He was woken by the dawn chorus; something he had never tired of. He fed the pigeon with a bit of the food he had been provided with and set about looking around the vicinity. He liked to live off the forest as much as possible and enjoyed it far more than he thought he would. Anyway, like the other snipers, he only had minimal rations, to reduce the amount he needed to carry. He found a few fruits he knew were safe and ate them with some of his rations; he washed it down with a couple of sips of water. Taking his bearings from the sun, he set off in the direction of his search area. He had been walking for a couple of days before he heard the sound of a lorry. He moved slowly until he could see the approaching convoy. There were far more than he had imagined and he couldn't understand why the reconnaissance planes hadn't seen this many vehicles on the move. He sat, hidden as the convoy went past. After they had gone, he moved slowly forward and kept under cover. He reached the track and was amazed at what he saw.

A single track road had been made through the forest. The branches of the trees had been cut back to allow the lorries to pass underneath without breaking cover. With the canopy above, they could not be spotted from the air. Walking down the road he saw that, every so often, there was a lay-by cut into the forest which was presumably for any breakdowns to pull into whilst they were repaired. He walked further up the road to check how far it went. After walking several miles he decided that it must travel in a fairly straight direction towards the front line. In places where the trees thinned, camouflage netting had been hung high up to prevent the road being seen. It was a colossal feat to get an entire road hidden like this. He wondered how many others snaked across the forest. Taking his bearings several times to check for accuracy, he wrote down the coordinates on a piece of paper, rolled it up and placed it carefully in the special case before attaching it to the pigeon's leg. He fed and watered the bird once more before finding a clear area in the trees and letting it go. All he could hope now was that the bird got safely back to base.

CHAPTER TEN

Jimmy watched his pigeon fly away; he couldn't see it for long as the forest blocked his vision. He hoped it would get back safely, but it was out of his hands now. He set off into the forest to make his way back, walking parallel to the road; he didn't want to walk on the road in case he was spotted. He then decided he was better off keeping away from the immediate area as he had no idea when the allies would decide to bomb it.

He knew he had a long hike ahead of him; it would take weeks, not days, to get back. Once he was a good distance from the road, he scraped out a hole in the forest floor and buried the pigeon box, covering it with loose soil and a thick layer of leaves. He wasn't expecting anyone to be looking for it, but wanted to take no chances. Once the road was bombed, the enemy would know someone had been in the area and Jimmy didn't want to leave any traces of his passing. For that same reason, he also made sure he buried all of the wrappings from his food. He set himself a steady pace and, after two days, came to the edge of the forest. The tunnel road split into three at this point. This was a clever ploy to disperse the convoys; sending them off at intervals in several directions and thus making the discovery of the covered road way harder for the allies.

Now, Jimmy would find it much harder to avoid discovery. With only small blocks of cover, he would be out in the open for a lot of the time. He had luck on his side for the first three nights, as there was a good moon, and he travelled at night. During the day he hid up in some of the clumps of trees dotting the area. He was glad of his tree climbing skills and slept in the branches above, well out of sight. As he moved nearer to the front line, things started to get more difficult. On one occasion, two aircraft flew overhead, firing Napalm into the clump of trees he was hiding in. They were allied planes and got a bit too close for comfort. Jimmy realised that he needed to be careful of attracting friendly fire as well as enemy fire on the remainder of his journey. Moving at night also had its hazards; twice he nearly stumbled over moon bears in the small forested areas. As he continued on his journey, he started to come across areas previously devastated by the war. The land had been destroyed, leaving large areas covered in craters with only small patches of cover. By now he was out of rations and any chance of living off the land was slim.

Even Jimmy's normally high moral was at a low ebb as he made his way across the battered landscape.

One night, as he was slowly moving across the area by moonlight, he spotted several Korean camps dotted across the land in front of him. He pushed on, making sure to go wide of the camps; at last he came to an area of trees and, entering into cover, he made his way into them until he found a place to hole up for a few hours. After a short rest, he moved on once more. He

Point the Finger of Blame

was keen to move in the daylight whilst he had cover. Going on, he came to a clearing with a log cabin to the side. Jimmy could see a couple of goats and chickens; there was also a well. He couldn't believe this had survived, with all the devastation around, but it must have been just away from the path of the front. Jimmy hadn't eaten or drunk for several days and made a bee-line for the well. In his desperate hunger and thirst, he hadn't given any thought as to whether any enemy would be at the cabin. As he got closer, he realised what he was doing but, by then, he was nearly there. He gave his position a fleeting thought but decided that he needed the water more. As he approached the well, a goose came round the corner, hissing at him. Shouting followed as the goose had alerted the cabin's occupants to an intruder; it was obviously kept as an alarm. A man came running out with a shotgun held high; he walked forward as if expecting a fox to be after his chickens. Jimmy held his hands up as the gun was pointed directly at him. Collapsing to the ground out of utter exhaustion and hunger, he didn't get the chance to regard anything of the man's appearance except his elderly stance. The man shouted for his wife who came out of the cabin. Between them, they dragged Jimmy indoors. When he came to, he was lying on the floor and the woman was trying to get him to drink some water. Jimmy managed to sit up and drink the water. He tried not to gulp it down too fast, as he knew he would only bring it back up again if he did. After he had drunk a little, the woman brought him some thin soup which he also drank. After a while, he got off the floor and sat in one of the chairs; he looked around the room. The couple's bed was in one corner with their chairs in the other. It was a small room and he could just make out a door that led to what looked like a kitchen come washhouse on the other side. The woman gestured towards a blanket on the floor and Jimmy understood that she wanted him to rest. He got down onto the blanket and fell asleep straight away. He slept for a full twenty four hours, waking only when the woman woke him for some more soup.

Jimmy got up and sat crossed legged on the floor; a plank that rested on some stout logs served as their table. The old man joined him and they all ate together. After they had eaten, the man pointed at the wall behind them. There against the wall stood his gun; Jimmy nodded his thanks. His empty rucksack was beside it. Jimmy stayed at the cabin for a week until he felt fit enough to make it back to base. He indicated to the couple that he was going to leave and they seemed to understand. The woman picked up his rucksack and put a bottle of water and some food inside before giving it to him. He was touched and wished he had something to give in return. He wondered why they had helped him, then thought that his parents would have probably done the same. It wasn't people who made wars but governments. With his energy renewed, he started back toward the allied lines.

Jimmy managed to avoid the enemy and crept back through his own lines without being spotted. Once there, he made his way to headquarters. His Canadian C.O was surprised to see him and arranged for him to go and to see the American general who had been in charge of his mission.

Jimmy was made to wait at least an hour before a sergeant beckoned him into the office.

Point the Finger of Blame

'You took your time getting back didn't you? Our man was back a week ago. Unfortunately, the rest got shot down in the helicopter. We received your coordinates and checked out the reference with a reconnaissance plane, but they found no sign of a road. I think you chickened out and gave us a false reference.'

This made Jimmy's blood boil but he knew not to answer back; being accused of cowardice upset him after all he had been though.

'Well, what have you got to say for yourself?' barked the General.

'Well Sir, I know what I saw and it was a road, well hidden under the tree canopy, with camouflage netting used to completely hide it from above. It was miles long; I followed its course on the way back until I ran out of cover. The road split into three.'

The General looked at Jimmy.

'I can't believe they could do that without our planes spotting work going on. You have an excellent record so I won't take any action against you until we get your story checked out. But, until I get proof, you're under house arrest.'

Jimmy's commanding officer came to see him when he got back to base. He knew Jimmy well and came to see what he could do; he was sure that the General had made a mistake. It took several days of reconnaissance with photography to give the General the proof he was looking for. They sent out a bombing mission and blitzed the area; once the canopy was damaged, the road could be clearly seen below.

The General sent for Jimmy.

DEREK SMITH

'Well, it looks like you were right. Think yourself lucky, it could have been a serious charge.'

With that he dismissed Jimmy who saluted and left the room; he was fuming that the General hadn't even apologised. But he realised that the war was going nowhere and it was drawing towards a stalemate, so the General had just taken his frustration out on him.

Despite all the allies' efforts, they continued to be pushed back towards the border. They lost ground on a daily basis until finally it was announced that the time came for the soldiers to return home. They didn't even have the satisfaction of winning the war; in fact, the whole war seemed a pointless exercise to many of the men. There was no official end to the war, but an armistice ensured a cessation of hostiles until a final peace settlement could be reached. A withdrawal of British and Commonwealth troops followed, but an American force would remain in South Korea. All in all, the men were only too happy to be leaving for home; they'd all had enough of fighting. Jimmy had seen lots of bloodshed and devastation of the countryside. One thing he would never forget was the old man and his wife. He had wanted to try to find them before he left but it hadn't been possible; he knew without doubt that the ordinary people caught up in these wars never wanted them. Wars might never even happen if only the little folk could have their say

CHAPTER ELEVEN

Jimmy had ended up spending three years in the army instead of the two he had expected. At least, that way, he wasn't going to be kept on the reserve list. He couldn't wait to get home and get his life back to normal. On the boats going back, none of the men were prepared for the return to a normal life. It was as if the government and the army were pretending the war hadn't happened. Jimmy's time in Korea had been spent living his life on a knife's edge, never knowing if each day would be his last; the peace left him with a feeling of anti-climax. He didn't seem to be able to relax and found himself spending most of his time alone. The army had been prepared to send him out to kill without thought and he would have liked to have talked things through with someone once it was all over; but, he had no idea who to approach.

The journey home was as tedious as the journey there had been. The only difference was the weariness of the men. They were all tired after spending so long in a war situation. At least they were heading home. A lot of the Canadians were career soldiers who would be staying in the army on their return. Still, all of them were looking forward to seeing their families and catching up with their lives. On their arrival in England, they all went back to the base in Bulford. Jimmy was then given a train ticket back up to Glasgow where he was to report and finally be discharged.

Jimmy felt happier back in his native country and, when he got back to the base, he reported as ordered. He was one of several hundred men all arriving at the same time. Along with the others, he had lots of paperwork to fill in. Then he was given his discharge papers, back pay and a ticket home. In Jimmy's case, this was Oban. He had hoped to be able to talk to someone about his future, but it seemed, now the army was finished with him, that they no longer cared what happened to him or any of the others.

Once he reached Oban, Jimmy decided to walk back to the estate. Despite the distance, he wanted to get a lung-full of clean Scottish air and soak in the views. He didn't have much to carry, just a kit bag and a couple of other items; he had been used to carrying them all over Korea so that was no hardship. It was so peaceful with no sounds of gun fire in the distance. It was great to be able to hear the familiar sounds of the wildlife that he remembered from his childhood. After a while, he saw a golden eagle soaring overhead and he stopped on a grassy hump to watch it. He sat there for over half an hour, entranced, before moving on once more.

Getting nearer the heart of the estate, he cut across country until he reached his father's favourite spot. Jimmy sat down once more to admire the view he had so missed. When he was in Korea, it was this view he remembered when thinking of his home. Getting up

Point the Finger of Blame

once more, he walked down the familiar path towards his home. It was just getting dusk as he reached the door. He stopped to listen and could hear both his parent's voices inside. He hadn't let them know he was back so it would be a complete surprise to them. A smile formed on his face as he lifted his hand and knocked on the door. He heard his father's footsteps come toward the door and, just before it opened, Jimmy turned so his father wouldn't see his face.

'What can I do for ...' his father started to say as the door opened.

Then, as Brian saw who was there, his voice changed to one of delight. 'Jimmy!'

Then louder: 'June! Jimmy's home!'

Jimmy found his father pulling him closer and, then, his mother was there hugging him; laughing and crying at the same time.

They were soon indoors with his mother fussing over him. Both his parents asked so many questions that he had a hard job answering one before they asked another. It was very late that night before Jimmy found himself in his own bed once more.

Although his parents had been overjoyed at getting him back safely, it was obvious within a very short time that Jimmy had returned home a changed man; not the same happy-go-lucky lad that had left three years before. His parents tried to talk to him about his time in Korea, but gave up when they realised he was trying to shut out the past. In fact, once he got back to Scotland, he spent most of the time wandering the hills alone. He did not seek the company of others, not even his family. They couldn't understand why he was so remote. Jimmy hadn't confided in them what he had done in the army and he avoided any questions as he knew his mother would be upset about what he had done. He was so moody that the locals soon learned to steer clear of him.

After he had been home for about a month, his mother asked him what he intended to do with his life now he'd left the army.

'I don't know Mum. The gunsmith's has closed so I can't go back there, the Laird doesn't need anyone and, with the rabbit population having myxamatosis, no one even needs them shot. Anyway, I've had enough of shooting to last me a lifetime.'

His mother looked at him, wondering what he had suffered in the war and what sights he must have seen.

'Why don't you go to the dance in Oban tomorrow night?'

Jimmy looked at his mother and smiled; he knew what she was trying to do. Thinking about it for a minute, he replied.

'Okay Mum, if it will keep you happy.'

So the next day, he caught the bus into town. On arriving at Oban, he walked around for a while and then went into the coffee bar. He soon felt out of place as it appeared, nowadays, it was frequented mainly by teenagers. Leaving the coffee bar, he headed toward the pub. Walking down the road, he saw a familiar face on the opposite side of the road. Jimmy crossed over and, sure enough, it was one of his old school friends. It turned out that his old friend was now married with a son. He had been lucky and spent his draft in the United Kingdom in the quartermaster's office. Jimmy had hoped to have someone to keep him company as he headed for the dance, but his old friend was hurrying home to his family. Jimmy headed up to the dance hall and stood by the door, looking in. There was quite a crowd in the hall; he spotted two girls he knew and headed towards them. They were soon chatting about old times. It seemed most of girls that Jimmy knew before he had gone to Korea were now married. He had just asked one of the girls for a dance when he felt a tap on his shoulder.

'Leave my girl alone.'

Jimmy turned round and came face to face with the Laird's nephew.

'Oh it's you, Jimmy. I heard you got demobbed and were back in the area.'

'Yes a few weeks ago. What about you?'

'I'm staying in. I've just been promoted and decided to have a night out celebrating with my friends.'

Jimmy turned around. There were three other men dressed in army uniforms behind Jonathan.

At this, one of the girls turned to Jonathan and said: 'I was just about to have a dance with Jimmy.'

'Oh no, you're not,' replied Jonathan. 'This dance is mine.'

'I don't think so, she's already agreed to dance with me,' said Jimmy.

Jonathan turned to the girls.

'Go and powder your noses. I'll have the next dance once I've sorted this out.'

He then turned toward his colleague.

'It looks like we need to teach Jimmy here to leave another man's girl alone, boys.'

Jimmy quickly sized up the situation and turned his back to the nearby wall. As the men lunged toward him, he fought back. Two of the men soon backed off and made themselves scarce. Even fighting two men, he soon had the upper hand and gave the two men a beating. Once the fight was over and neither of the men came back for more, Jimmy walked out of the hall. After tidying himself up, he caught a bus back home, deciding it wasn't worth all the bother just for a dance or two.

After Jimmy had left the hall, it was found out that Jonathan was so badly beaten that he needed hospital treatment. His mate wasn't much better. The next morning, the police arrived at Jimmy's parents; he was arrested for violent disorder and taken back to Oban police station. On Monday morning, he was taken before the court; he was quickly found guilty of aggravated bodily harm, fined one hundred pounds, and bound over to keep the peace for twelve months. On returning home, he was greeted by his mother. She looked like she had been crying.

'Your father wants to talk to you; he's round the back of the sheds.'

Jimmy went and found his father.

'Alright lad, tell me what happened.'

Jimmy told his father, leaving nothing out. He realised that his actions must have put his father in an awkward position. After telling him everything, including the court's decision, he waited whilst his father thought things through.

'I'm sorry lad but the Laird called me up to the big house. He doesn't want you round the place. He hasn't got any kids of his own, as you know, and he intends to leave the place to his nephew. I'm sorry but this has been your mother's home and my livelihood; it's difficult for us all but I'm afraid you can't stay around here

Point the Finger of Blame

anymore. I'm really sorry, I understand you had to defend yourself, but we've no choice. At our age, I'd never get another job like this so I've got to go along with what the Laird's ordered. After all, it was his nephew who ended up in hospital.'

Brian was obviously very upset by what had happened.

'Look lad, the Laird understands his nephew's involvement. He knows Jonathan is no angel. He told me that you should look up a friend of his; you've got a job waiting for you at Coventry with Wimpey's, the builders. It will tide you over until you get yourself settled somewhere.'

Jimmy realised his father understood and probably approved of him standing up for himself but he had to consider his wife. Jimmy also realised, at his father's time of life, it wouldn't be easy if he had to find another job. It also explained why his mother had looked like she'd been crying.

He turned to his dad once more and said: 'Don't worry, I understand. I'll get my things and go straight away; no point in dragging it out. I'll keep in touch and perhaps come back for a short visit once things have quietened down. Look after yourself and Mum. Sorry it worked out this way but I would have probably moved on anyway, so don't feel bad. The war's changed us all. Maybe a fresh start is what I need.'

With that, he shook his father's hand and walked back to the house. Quickly going upstairs he packed his few belongings and went and said goodbye to his mother. She was crying again and unable to speak, but she gave him a big hug. Within the hour, he had left his family home. With a forced smile, he waved goodbye to his parents once again. Jimmy was soon on the bus back to Oban, and then caught a train to Coventry. Thinking back on the events of the past few days, he couldn't believe his luck. If it had been anyone other than Jonathan, he felt he would still be sitting at home now. He didn't worry for himself but he was upset about the effect it'd had on his parents, particularly his mother. He hated being the cause of her crying. He hoped that, one day, he would be able to make it up to her. However, he thought it was unlikely that he would return for a long time, if ever. After all, when Jonathan became the Laird, he wouldn't be welcome. He was in two minds whether to go for the job in Coventry but was realistic enough to know he needed a job as soon as possible. Once he had a bit of money together, he could always move on.

CHAPTER TWELVE

After arriving at Coventry, he went straight to the taxi rank and asked the cab driver to take him to the address his father had given him. On arrival he found a large building site, far bigger than he had been expecting. From the taxi window, he had seen several areas of overgrown ruins still remaining from World War Two. They brought back memories of the war he had left behind him. He wondered how the Koreans would cope with the aftermath. Getting out of the taxi, he paid the driver and went toward a group of three caravans. One had a sign saying 'Site Office'. He knocked on the door.

A gruff voice from inside said 'come in'.
Inside was a rugged looking man in his fifties.
'I'm Jim McLeod. I think you're expecting me.'
'Bert Whistle, site agent'.

Jimmy shook the huge hand that was coming towards him. He winced as his hand was crushed in a vice-like grip. Bert had a twinkle in his eye as he saw Jimmy's reaction.

DEREK SMITH

'I had the call to say you where coming lad. You aren't a builder are you son? Your hands are too soft, although I'd say you're not a stranger to hard work.'

Before Bert could say anything else, Jimmy replied.

'No, I've just spent three years in Korea.'

'Guess that weren't no holiday camp.' Bert's voice took on a more respectful tone. 'Look, you can start tomorrow morning. But, first things first, go across to the canteen and get yourself fed. If you've got no money, I'll give you a sub. Your wages will be for a labourer since you've no previous experience. You'll work a week in hand.'

'Thanks, but I'm okay for now. I couldn't spend much in Korea. That was the only good thing about the place,' he said with a grin.

'Allan Kirby runs the canteen. If you ask him, he'll probably know someone with a spare bed in the area. Just tell him I sent you over.'

With that, Jimmy left the office and headed straight to the canteen. He hadn't realised just how hungry he was until Bert had mentioned food. On arriving at the canteen, he was greeted by a short thin man with a soft Irish accent. After introducing himself, Jimmy soon finished off a large fry-up and then asked Allan about a room. He was pleased when Allan told him that his lodger had just left and he had a spare bed that Jimmy could use. It was in one of the other caravans. Allan took him across to see it. The caravan was cosy looking. It had a table and two chairs together, with a small cooker and a sink. Two doors led to two small bedrooms.

Point the Finger of Blame

'The toilet and washing facilities are in the cabin round the back. It will be five bob a week up front,' said Allan.

'Your room's small but has a bunk bed. You can use the top bunk for your things and the bottom to sleep in.'

As there was no mattress on the top bunk, this seemed rather obvious. Jimmy just nodded his head and threw his bags on the top bunk, after quickly accepting the offer. It would save him looking around for anything and Allan seemed a nice enough sort. Handing over the first week's rent, he soon settled in. He was pleased to have found something so easily and so near his work. With the details settled, Allan left him to it and went back to the canteen. Jimmy unpacked his radio and settled down to listen to it. His thoughts soon drifted and he started to think about how Britain was changing. One of the first things he had noticed on arriving home was that the rabbit population had been wiped out by myxamatosis and, with it, many of the pest control men's jobs had gone. This also removed a cheap food source for the country folk. The King had also died whilst Jimmy was away and a new young Queen was on the throne. While he was travelling to Coventry, and especially since his arrival, he realised just how much damage still remained from World War Two. It wasn't something he'd thought about much. He hadn't gone to any of the badly bombed cities before going to Korea and, although the dock yard in Scotland had taken a pounding, the countryside hadn't seen much of the war. Maybe an odd bomber unloading spare bombs before flying back to Germany but, at the estate, they had suffered no damage.

DEREK SMITH

The task of rebuilding the country was underway but it was a huge task and he was about to join that effort. Later that afternoon, Allan came back and they had a cup of tea and a good natter. They went down to the local pub for a couple of pints and a game of darts before going back for a night's rest.

The next morning, he got ready for his first day in the building trade. As luck would have it, he still had some of his combat clothes and boots. He got dressed and headed for the office to get his instructions for the day. Joining a group of men, they headed for the far end of the site. Today they were working on demolishing the remains of some bombed out buildings; it was to be a site for a new block of flats. Housing was still very short and many people were waiting to be properly housed. World War Two had caused so much devastation that the building trade had still not managed to keep up with demand. The nearby Leyland car plant was desperate for homes for their workers and flats were the quickest way of providing the homes required. Jimmy took to the work well, after some initial muscle pain at the hard physical work. He found the men on the site hard but fair. They came from all walks of life and, as long as you put in a good days work, you were accepted; no one asked questions or seemed to care what you had done in the past.

The weeks flew by with hard work and a feeling of comradeship that built up in the team. They had lots of laughs and the jokes fell thick and fast. Jimmy soon found out that you needed to have a fairly thick skin as the jokes were as much about people as anything. If anyone had a mishap or made a mistake they would be ribbed unmercifully. The evenings were spent chatting

Point the Finger of Blame

to Allan. The couple got on well and Jimmy would tell him about some of his experiences in Korea. He told Allan of the swarms of Chinese soldiers who came over the border to fight and the men who died to stop them. He spoke with bitterness about the futility as the war had ended in stalemate. Jimmy felt that the people back home never knew what went on. Allan had fought in the Second World War but agreed that at least they had won; thus, the population at home had some understanding of the horrors of war. The buildings they were demolishing had been housing to many before the war. The bombing raids over Coventry had meant that those at home had felt some of the horrors war could bring. Except for those who had family serving in the forces, the Korean War hadn't really had much impact on the ordinary folk in Britain.

Jimmy threw everything he had into this new style of work, determined to make some sort of success out of the enforced changes into his plans. He still had hopes of going back to Scotland one day and finding a job in game-keeping but, for now, this was his future; he needed to earn himself some money. It was heavy, dirty work, day after day, clearing away the demolished houses. He was used to hard work; but, he had aches in muscles he didn't know he had before and the calluses on his hands from using his gun were all in the wrong places. He found that he was getting blisters to start with but he persevered. They were soon making headway in clearing the site for the new buildings. He thought again how different this job was than anything else he had done before. Game-keeping would have been his ideal job but he had also enjoyed his time with the gunsmith. Even the army had its good points, although he had never for one moment thought of staying in once his time was up. He supposed it would be different in peace time but, then again, peace never seemed to last long.

But, in the building trade, he found himself working in a group of men, which none of his other jobs had really given him. They came from all walks of life and nationalities. There were Poles, Irish and Scots, all with different tales to tell. Some had fought in the Second World War and some in Korea, like him. One of the men told him he had been in Korea; he had been captured along with six hundred others when they had been defending a hill. This brought back memories for Jimmy as he had heard about it when he was out there. He tried to forget the war as much as possible and avoided telling anyone that he had been a sniper. Instead, if anyone pushed him, he said he fought with the Canadians - which was true as far as it went.

It seemed to Jimmy that the building site was full of men who were nomads; travelling from one job to another, never seeming to stay anywhere very long. They seemed not to have a care in the world and, although hard workers, they had no respect for discipline or authority. If anyone upset them, they just left and went on to another site. Some of the men were as tough as nails, as Jimmy soon found out. One night, he went to a local pub for a drink. Allan had stayed behind as he had the cookers to clean. Jimmy found himself next to an Irishman. He had worked with him on one occasion; he was a big and very fit man who always answered to the name of Paddy. A fight broke out at the other end of the bar and, before long, everyone was joining in. It was just like a fight from a

Point the Finger of Blame

Wild West film, with bodies flying everywhere. Paddy turned toward Jimmy and, without a word, grabbed him and landed a punch. Jimmy tried to defend himself but to no avail; then, Paddy picked him up and threw him over the bar. He landed heavily and hit his head on the shelving. He staggered to his feet and fell backwards through the swinging doors which led to where the landlord stored the real ale barrels. He landed on the floor and sat up dazed, feeling lucky to be out of the fight. Once he got his breath back, he was even more pleased to be out of the fight. He spotted four beer barrels all with taps attached and a row of clean glasses.

Whilst the fight continued in the bar, Jimmy decided to continue his drinking in peace. He helped himself to a pint from the first barrel and sat drinking happily while the fight continued in the next room. Sometime later he heard the police arrive and, after a while, it all went quiet once more. All he could hear was the landlord clearing up; then, he realised that the landlord was coming toward the backroom. Jimmy felt a bit dizzy and slipped off his perch on the bench, sliding to the floor. He had a skin full, having drunk quite a bit from each barrel. He had never got used to drinking much, so he didn't need to have many pints to feel the effects. With that, the landlord walked through the swinging doors.

'What the hell are you doing in here?' he demanded.

'I've had a bash on the head and feel very woozy,' Jimmy slurred in reply.

The landlord walked toward him and looked him over. On Jimmy's head he noticed a bruise as large as an egg, where he had hit the shelf after being thrown over the bar.

'Try and stand up, lad,' said the landlord, giving him a helping hand.

He was very unsteady on his feet. The landlord put it down to the blow on the head, but Jimmy knew better.

'Don't call an ambulance, I'll be okay,' muttered Jimmy, as the landlord seemed to be getting concerned about his unsteady stance.

The landlord wanted to get on. The last thing he needed was to have to wait around for the ambulance to come and, seeing Jimmy was able to walk, he helped him to the door and watched him stagger down the pavement. He was relieved that Jimmy appeared well as he'd had enough and just wanted to clear up so he could go to bed. Jimmy staggered back to the caravan and managed to creep in without waking Allan. He fell on the bed and was asleep as soon as his head hit the pillow. He hadn't even taken off his clothes. In the morning, he was woken up by Allan.

'Come on Jimmy or you'll be late for work. You must have had a good time to sleep on.'

Jimmy winced. He had a headache and a half. Lifting his hand to his forehead, he felt the bruise and winced. He wasn't sure if it was the beer or the bruise that was causing the headache.

Allan saw the bruise and asked what had happened.

'Oh, there was a bit of a fight last night and Paddy threw me over the bar.'

'I should have warned you about that. Never stand anywhere near Paddy if there's any sort of fight in the offing; he's apt to throw people around.'

Point the Finger of Blame

'Now you tell me,' said Jimmy. 'It's a bit late now, but I will remember in future.'

He got up, had a wash, and changed into his working clothes; he got his kit together and set off down to the site with a mug of tea in his hand.

On the site the men, including those men that had been fighting the night before, were laughing and joking about the previous evening. It seemed that they had all enjoyed themselves; they obviously played as hard as they worked. Several had noticeable bruises and others were a bit stiffer than normal but there was no rancour between them, even if they had found themselves on different sides during the fight. As long as the management of the site weren't upset, the men were able to have their fun. Paddy asked Jimmy where he had got to the previous evening.

Jimmy laughed: 'After you threw me over the bar I fell into the backroom and stayed there drinking while you lot carried on fighting.'

Paddy laughed. 'The boss is going down to the pub and paying for the damage, so no charges will be passed. But we will all have the money docked out of our wages, including you! So you still get to pay for your beer. Good night though, weren't it?'

'If you say so Paddy, I won't argue with you.'

Paddy laughed and got back to his work.

Jimmy still wished his head wasn't thumping so much. He was glad when the day was over and he could get a good sleep.

A couple of weeks later and the men had finished clearing the site for the start of the new building. An official ceremony had been arranged for the start of the next phase. The council staff, architects and the company's management came to the opening. The men, including Jimmy, were told to make themselves scarce until after the opening. The officials who attended the ceremony were given a free lavish buffet after the ceremony; the local television company had arrived to film the opening. At about three o'clock, they had finished and left the site; the workers were told they could finish what food was left. The men all refused as they felt they were being treated like animals, being fed the scraps after all they had done, all the hard graft, even if they weren't invited to the party. The episode caused friction between the workers and management but, with the same company having most of the contracts, most of the men remained on site for the next phase.

CHAPTER THIRTEEN

With the new phase started, Jimmy was soon learning a new set of skills. The site plans needed to be set out and there were wooden pegs everywhere. The foundations were soon being dug and all the ground works were starting. Then, it wasn't long before brickwork was going up and the beginnings of the flats could clearly be seen. The weeks turned into months, with no let up in the work. Allan and Jimmy became firm friends, spending much of their spare time together either betting on the horses, drinking at the local pub or meeting up with the local women. The pair enjoyed some of their days off exploring the area in Allan's old van.

With the flats nearly finished and the landscaping well underway, Jimmy was with the group building a wall around what was to be a park area for the flats. They were completing the last bit of the wall when Bert asked Jimmy and Allan if they would go with him to his next job. It was for a different firm called Pearce and Son. They agreed and, as the site was just down the street, it was an easy task to move the cabins and canteen to their new site. It wasn't long before the couple had settled in to the new job. As neither of them had seen their families for some time, their relationship was almost brotherly. When the site shut down for the summer break, they decided to go on holiday. Allan had seen an advert for a holiday camp called "Butlins" and they soon booked their places. The camp was in the West Country and they travelled down in Allan's car. The pair had a great time, chatting up the female redcoats and enjoying the entertainment every night. The cost of the holiday included three meals a day and Allan found it a nice change not having to do the cooking. There were quite a few young and unattached girls at the site and they soon struck up a friendship with a couple from London, who were also on holiday. They all knew nothing would come of it but enjoyed themselves just the same. Jimmy even sat down one morning and sent a postcard to his parents. It was the first time he had contacted them since he had left, but they knew he wasn't one for writing.

It was like heaven on earth to the men. When the holiday finished, they found themselves a lot poorer, but far happier. As time passed, the horrors of the Korean War were being pushed to the back of Jimmy's mind. However, he still found himself thinking of his previous life in Scotland and often wondered what would have happened in his life if he had been able to stay there.

Getting back to work, Jimmy soon got back into the swing of things. He had become a first rate digger driver and Allan was making a great success of the canteen. They continued to work the sites across the area. As they sat reminiscing one evening, Jimmy realised that he had been working in the building trade for over three years. Where had the time gone?

Point the Finger of Blame

One lunch time, he was sitting eating his midday meal in the canteen; a lorry pulled up outside and two men came in. One was a giant of a man; he ordered a meal and coffee for both of them. Allan made the coffee and put it on the counter.

'I'll bring your meal over when it's ready. That will be one pound please.'

With that, the big man leaned over the counter and grabbed Allan by the lapels. He dragged him over the counter.

Without waiting to see what else happened, Jimmy jumped to his feet. The other man moved toward Jimmy who threw a punch that floored the man. Jimmy then set about the bigger man; he had the element of surprise and caught the man totally off guard. Throughout, Jimmy didn't lose his cool. He didn't like to see bullying in any shape or form and wasn't about to let Allan be attacked in this way. Jimmy gave the big man a thrashing and despite the size difference his opponent hardly landed a blow in return. It wasn't long before the big man was knocked out. The second man by now had called an ambulance and the pair were soon taken to the local hospital.

Later that afternoon, Bert Whistle approached Jimmy. It appeared that his opponent had lost several teeth, fractured a cheek bone and suffered concussion.

'Sorry lad. I heard what happened from the lads but you beat up the wrong man. He's the boss's son. I've been told to sack you and you need to leave the site immediately.'

Bert didn't look very happy to be getting rid of Jimmy.

'If I were you, I'd leave as soon as you can. They're going to press charges.'

With that, he gave Jimmy an envelope. 'Here's the money you're owed and a bit more on top. Go on lad, get going. Sorry to lose you.'

With that, Bert turned and went back toward the office. Jimmy cursed his bad luck; what was it about him and boss's sons? He picked up his tools and went toward the caravan to collect the rest of his gear.

On entering, he found Allan sitting on the lower bunk.

'I know it wasn't your fault Jimmy, you were trying to help me. But, I've been warned off from being a witness for you. They said you wouldn't be with me 24/7 to protect me. I'm real sorry but I can't risk it; I've got everything I have tied up in the canteen and vans. I've got no choice.'

Jimmy knew that Allan wasn't a fighter and didn't blame him for what had happened.

'Don't worry Allan; it was time I moved on anyway.'

With that, he turned and started to collect his belongings. Before he could leave, the police arrived and arrested him.

It wasn't long before he was up before the local magistrate; his solicitor told him he had little chance of avoiding a guilty verdict. They knew about his previous problems in Scotland. The judge listened to both sides of the evidence. As Jimmy had no one to back his story, the judge wasted little time in pronouncing sentence.

'McLeod, it appears you are unable to control your temper. Due to this, I have no alternative but to give you a custodial sentence of three months.'

Point the Finger of Blame

As he was taken back to the cells he was met by Allan, who had been watching from the galley.

'Sorry Jimmy. If you want me to, I'll look after your things whilst you're inside.'

Jimmy nodded his assent and walked on back to the cells.

It wasn't long before he was transferred to prison. His spell in prison didn't worry him; he'd had worse treatment in the army. He was only glad he wasn't in close contact with his parents; they would have been mortified to know he had been in trouble again.

He was taken to Bristol to complete his sentence. Horfield was an old Victorian prison and often overcrowded. Jimmy kept to himself during his time there. He kept his nose down and managed to stay out of the many fights that occurred. He hated being shut up and wanted to get out as soon as he could. He didn't mind the regime as such but hated not being able to get outside for long walks. He found time dragged, but he had time to think and brood about his life. He would have liked to have gone back to Scotland but felt he would only bring more trouble to his parents. It seemed to him that people brought him nothing but trouble. He wasn't sure what to do once he'd left prison, but he would need to do something.

CHAPTER FOURTEEN

He did his time and, when the day of his release came, was taken to a room where he was met by a social worker and Allan. Jimmy was surprised to see Allan there; he hadn't expected to see him until he got to the site to collect his belongings. The social worker told Jimmy that Allan had explained what happened.

'As you served your country well in Korea, I've managed to get you one of the new council flats in Coventry so you will have somewhere to live. You have the British Legion to thank for that; they are useful in cases like these.'

Jimmy was glad he at least had a roof over his head. The rent was reasonable and it gave him time to work out what he was going to do next. He shook Allan's hand and gave him a pat on the shoulder. He didn't blame Allan; he hadn't had a choice, no more than his father had years before. It seemed that the odds would always be stacked against you, unless you had enough money to buy your way out of trouble. Allan was now working in Bath on a site for the same company; so, after handing over Jimmy's belongings, he said his goodbyes and left.

Point the Finger of Blame

Jimmy had lost a good friend because of bullying; just as he had lost contact with his parents because of the power money gave to people. It seemed to him that money gave you power, no matter whether you were right or wrong. Jimmy felt bitter. He had spent three years of his life fighting in these people's name, just to come home, spend time in prison and get a criminal record because of dishonest men. The social worker told him there was a road sweeper's job going for Coventry council if he wished to apply. Jimmy's first thought had been to re-enlist in the army but he was quickly told that, now he had a criminal record, he would not be accepted.

Jimmy decided to apply for the council job; it would give him the chance to sort himself out and put money in his pocket. With the backing of the social worker, he was given the job and started work. Jimmy was given a brush and cart, and given a patch of the town to keep clean. He was to look after all the pavements and keep a local park clear of litter. He was surprised to find it was the very park he had helped to build the wall around three months earlier. The plants had grown well and looked like they had been there for some time. Nature was amazing at recovering whatever man did to it. Although the job was a menial one, Jimmy took great pride in his work and spent much of his free time tending the flowers and shrubs. At least with this job he was his own boss and didn't have to deal with other people too much. He gradually became at ease with his world once again.

One morning, several months later, he was amazed and upset to find the park had been trashed overnight. The benches had been broken and the flowers trodden into the ground. There were broken bottles and litter thrown everywhere. He reported the damage to the council and, after the area had been inspected by the council and the police, he set about trying to put right what he could. It appeared that a group of students from the nearby university had been seen in the park late the previous night. They had been caught, following a tip off, by one of the locals.

Jimmy heard no more about the outcome of the tip off; so one day, when he bumped into one of the arresting officers, he asked him what had happened to the students.

'Sorry lad. They were taken to court but got off with a warning,' replied the policeman.

It appeared that they were well represented as one of the boy's fathers was a local businessman.

It seemed, yet again to Jimmy, that there was one law for the rich and one for the poor. The students hadn't even been made to pay for the damages they had caused. It wasn't long after this that Jimmy was in the park one evening, when he spotted a group of students on one of the benches. The group had several bottles of drink with them. Jimmy watched as one of the young men threw an empty bottle onto the path, where it smashed; another threw his empty bottle into the flower bed. Jimmy walked up to the group and politely asked the student to pick up the bottle from the flower bed. One of the lads got mouthy so Jimmy singled him out; he grabbed the lads arm and forced it up behind the lads back.

'Pick up the bottle,' he demanded.

At the same time he pushed the lad down toward the empty bottle. Two of his mates tried to kick Jimmy but they were no match for him. The lad he was holding started to cry; the other ran off and found a policeman. This time, luck was on Jimmy's side; a lady walking her dog had watched what had happened and explained to the policeman as he arrived. The matter was reported to the council and Jimmy was asked to report to his boss. In the office, Jimmy was reprimanded.

'You used unnecessary force on these lads; the youngest was only seventeen and the oldest eighteen.'

Jimmy quickly replied, 'I wasn't much older than that when I was fighting in Korea; if you're old enough to be fighting for your country, you should be old enough to be responsible for your actions.'

'These lads don't come from a working class background, they are privileged members of society; the one you manhandled was a banker's son.'

Before his boss could say any more, Jimmy butted in: 'Does that mean they don't have to behave? If they're privileged then surely they should know right from wrong.'

'Look, sorry, but the boy's parents have a lot of influence in this town and they don't want their boys manhandled in this way. Like it or not, that's how it is. There's no point in arguing anymore; you've gone too far and the council no longer needs your services. You're fired and, before you argue, the only reason you're not being charged is because Lady Whitley spoke up for you.'

'Who's Lady Whitley?'

'The lady in the park who witnessed the event; she seemed to think you were in the right but I'm afraid it didn't do you any good in the end.'

DEREK SMITH

'Well it's nice to know that someone has the guts to speak up against that lot.'

Jimmy left the building, yet again out of work. Because of his record, it was getting harder to find jobs; he managed to find just enough casual work to pay the rent and keep the wolf from the door. He did think of moving on to find work; but, he had his flat and, as a single man, he would find it difficult to find another. Jimmy found that, with time to himself, he was spending many hours in the local parks, watching birds and feeding them the scraps of bread he had left. He would sit for hours, patiently watching the wildlife. He was thrilled when he managed to get one of the squirrels to eat out of his hand. He knew how to identify it as it had one ear darker than the other. Feeding the squirrel became a regular part of his routine and one he looked forward to. Then, one day, Jimmy found the squirrel dead under a tree; it appeared to have been beaten to death with a blood-covered stick which he found by the body. Jimmy was upset at the cruelty of what had happened; he had killed animals himself, even humans, but always quickly and never without reason. In a way, he blamed himself for making the animal trust humans enough to let them get close.

About a week later, while he was walking home through the park, he saw the same group of students on the benches ahead of him. As he walked past, the boy who he had manhandled shouted out.

'Seen your pet squirrel lately?'

Jimmy knew straight away that the lad had been responsible for the animal's brutal death. He said nothing but kept walking. He wasn't prepared to go back to prison just because of a loud mouthed kid.

CHAPTER FIFTEEN

Jimmy was looking for a new outlet. He still fed the birds but the incident had spoiled the park for him. One of the people from the flats gave him an old fishing rod, together with some other bits and pieces. Word had got out that he'd lost his job trying to keep the area nice for the locals, so he had received several offers of help from his neighbours. He had always loved fishing; the solitude seemed to suit him and it brought back happy memories of earlier days. He had even made a special carrying case for his rod out of a piece of sewer pipe. Sometimes, he'd catch the bus out of town and camp out by the canal overnight; in many ways it reminded him of his army days. He didn't need to take much with him as he could catch his supper and easily sleep under the stars. On one of his many visits, he struck up a friendship with a young lad of about twelve years old. The lad approached him as he was fishing.

He introduced himself: 'Hi, I'm Colin. Can I sit here and fish? It's my normal place.'

Colin didn't have much in the way of fishing kit but was quite happy sitting on the canal bank with his small rod. They sat together for several hours, hardly talking at all, just enjoying their fishing. Before dusk, Colin left for home.

After that, they often met and would sit all day fishing together. Jimmy gradually got to know a bit about his young companion. It seemed Colin's dad worked long hours and he didn't get to see much of him. He lived on one of the council estates not far from the river. Colin seemed to spend most of his weekends and holidays down by the canal, quietly fishing. As they got to know one another better, Jimmy gradually passed on fishing tips to the lad and, sometimes, he let him use his own spare rod for a while. They would sit about 20 yards apart and fish all day. One day when they were fishing, a steward came along and asked Colin if he could see his fishing licence. Colin admitted he didn't have one and the steward grabbed the rod from the boy's hand and started to pull the boy to his feet, scaring the lad. Jimmy stood up and walked toward the couple; reaching out, he took the rod from the steward's hand. The steward looked round and realised he was not just dealing with a small boy; seeing the look on Jimmy's face, he backed off.

'I'll be back. If I find you here again, there will be trouble.'

With that, he went off down the path. Colin was worried and said he had better not come again but Jimmy told him not to worry.

'I've got a licence. If he says anything again, tell him you're with me.'

This seemed to reassure Colin and he settled back down to fish once more.

The next weekend, Jimmy and Colin were sitting fishing when the steward came along the towpath, at the side of the canal, on his bike. Just as the steward went past, Jimmy flipped his rod back, catching the handle end in the wheel of the bike sending the steward flying over the handlebars. Jimmy stood up and retrieved his rod, checking it for damage.

Looking at the steward on the ground, he said: 'Sorry, I didn't see you coming.'

Both Jimmy and the steward knew it was a lie but nothing more was said. After that, neither Colin nor Jimmy saw the steward again.

A couple of weeks later, Jimmy set out one morning to spend a couple of days on the canal, at his usual spot, where he knew won't be disturbed. Jimmy was soon settled and spent the day fishing; he was joined by Colin for a couple of hours but, about ten o'clock, Colin stood up.

'I've got to go shopping with my mum for some new school trousers this afternoon.'

'Okay, see you next week maybe,' replied Jimmy.

He carried on fishing and, as darkness began to fall, sorted out a fire to cook his supper. Lying on his back, he looked up at the night sky. Out of town he could spot far more of the constellations; the street lights made star gazing much harder. In Korea he had used the stars for direction as much as his compass and, although he now saw different star patterns, he could enjoy just looking at the sky. Now, it wasn't a matter of life or death as it had been in Korea. It was even better as he managed to catch a fish for his supper and it was free.

Next morning, he decided to make his way home. He had enjoyed himself but decided to go back and see

DEREK SMITH

if he could find a bit of work. When he got there, he found the local policeman standing outside the door.

'Hello Jimmy. We've been waiting for you since yesterday; come with me and bring all your stuff with you, your coming down the station with me.'

'What's up now?' said Jimmy.

The policeman wouldn't say. He suggested that it would be in Jimmy's best interests if he went without trouble. Once they reached the station, he was taken into one of the interview rooms where he was met by Detective Sergeant Birch. Looking round, Jimmy noticed there were no windows in the room; just a table and two chairs.

'Sit down Jimmy,' said the detective.

He also noticed there was a young police woman already sat behind the desk.

'You know why you're here, don't you?'

'No, I don't. I asked but wasn't told anything,' said Jimmy.

He couldn't believe he hadn't even been able to put his things indoors before being taken to the station. He felt grubby and had been looking forward to having a good wash when he got home.

'There's been a murder in the park; a student has been killed. Before we go any further, I need to caution you and ask if you want a solicitor.'

Jimmy declined a solicitor; they had never helped in the past and, anyway, he had nothing to hide. After he was cautioned, the questioning started.

'Where were you yesterday?'

'I've been fishing on the canal out by the village of Nettleton. I spent the night out there. I often go fishing; it passes the time and I like the countryside.'

Point the Finger of Blame

The detective sergeant wasn't convinced. 'Did anyone see you there?'

'I spoke to a couple of people on the barges as they went by but, otherwise, no. I like to find quiet spots.'

Jimmy wasn't going to tell them about Colin; he didn't want the lad to have to face questioning from the police. Jimmy was questioned for several hours, with the sergeant going over and over the same things. Even if he had done anything, the questioning wouldn't have achieved much. Jimmy had undertaken training in the army for just such questioning, in case he had been captured. What's more, he knew he was innocent and they weren't about to torture him, like the Koreans may have done. Jimmy thought it wouldn't be much longer before he would be able to leave; they didn't appear to have any evidence. He'd gleaned that much. In fact, he had probably got more out of the sergeant than he did from Jimmy.

After twelve hours, he was released.

'Can I have my fishing gear back?' Jimmy asked the detective.

'No, it's going through forensic tests. Once it's given the all clear, we will let you know and you can collect it then.'

Looking Jimmy straight in the eye, the detective sergeant said: 'I know you did it. I'll get you before I've finished.'

Jimmy turned and walked away; he knew it wasn't worth saying anymore. On the way home, he stopped and picked up a paper.

On the front page the headline read: 'Stockbroker's son murdered with a blunt instrument through his left eye.'

He didn't read anymore then; he would wait until he got home.

After he had made himself a cup of tea, he settled down in his favourite chair and picked up the paper. Jimmy wondered if the detective had thought he'd used his fishing rod to kill the boy; or, perhaps his penknife. That was why they had kept his fishing tackle. Looking down at his thumb, where he had caught his fishing hook earlier, he knew the only traces of blood they would find would be the fish's and his. He read the article through. It appeared that the student that had been killed was one of the individuals he'd had a run-in with before. Jimmy could see why the police thought he might be involved but, then, with the attitude of the student, he felt he wouldn't be the only one who had a reason to dislike him.

A couple of days later, a local police constable returned his fishing tackle, having found nothing to incriminate him. After getting Jimmy to check his property and getting him to sign for it, the constable turned on him.

'You'll be a marked man now. Detective Sergeant Birch thinks you are guilty and he doesn't give up easily.'

Looking straight at the policeman, Jimmy shrugged his shoulders.

'I'm innocent, so what the detective thinks doesn't bother me.'

Without saying more, the constable turned and left. Jimmy put his fishing gear away before starting to get his breakfast.

CHAPTER SIXTEEN

Jimmy tried to carry on as normal. The newspapers reported no more developments and gradually the fuss started to die down in the neighbourhood. But, Jimmy was aware that he was often watched as he carried on with his normal routine. His army training, so long a matter of life and death, meant he was aware of being watched. It didn't bother him much but sometimes, just for devilment, he would give his watchers the slip and go off for a long walk. Other times, he would lead them a merry dance and walk all over the town for no reason; just to keep his followers busy. After a while, the watching stopped, with just the occasional appearance of a local policeman near his home.

Jimmy started to fish again as well at his normal place; he often went back to the canal near Nettleton and it was there, about midnight, when Jimmy heard someone approaching. It was Detective Birch and a uniformed constable. Detective Birch sat down on the bank next to Jimmy. The constable remained on his feet a couple of yards away. With heavy sarcasm in his voice, the detective turned to Jimmy.

'I suppose you've been here all day?'

'Since dinner time,' replied Jimmy.

'And what time was dinner?'

'About noon.'

'I suppose you can prove it.'

Jimmy grinned and replied. 'Ask that swan over there,' he pointed across to the other bank. 'She's been sitting on her nest all the time and, what's more, she's been keeping a close eye on me. I thought she was working for you.'

This niggled the detective; he stood up and, looking down at Jimmy, he said: 'You best come with me, smarty pants.'

The constable had moved closer. Jimmy stood up and collected his belongings. It was obvious to him that he would be going, so he made no fuss. He knew he'd find out soon enough what they wanted.

Jimmy was taken once more to the same interview room at the local police station. Again, he was asked if he wanted a solicitor and, again, he refused. After reading him his rights, he was questioned. This time, they kept him for thirty six hours before releasing him. It appeared that there had been another murder. A lawyer had been out jogging in the park and had been murdered using the same method.

When Jimmy got back to his flat, he found a police constable outside. He turned and left as Jimmy approached. Opening the door, he found that the whole flat had been ransacked. It looked as if he had been burgled but he knew that the damage was due to the search the police had undertaken. He sat down in his chair and looked at the mess around him. After about ten minutes, he shook his head, stood, and started to tidy up. He was angry and he felt that they should be

Point the Finger of Blame

more careful with other people's possessions. He was tired and ached all over; he wondered if he was getting a cold. That was the last thing he needed, so he gave up and decided to get a bit of sleep. When he woke up, he still had aches and pains. So, in order to get moving and stop himself feeling stiff, he went down to the corner shop and bought a paper and a pint of milk. The shopkeeper was normally very chatty but today he just seemed to want Jimmy out as quickly as possible. This suited Jimmy; he had a lot of thinking to do. When he got home and opened the paper, he understood the shopkeeper's hurry. He had been named as a suspect for the two murders. This annoyed him; the police had no evidence and yet his name was all over the papers. He'd never find any work now. Jimmy sat down and wrote a letter; picking it up, he left the flat and headed down town. Even on that short journey, he noticed several people staring at him. Going into the police station, he asked to see the officer in charge. After waiting for a short time, a uniformed officer came to the desk. Jimmy handed him the letter he had written earlier.

'I want you to take this and hand it in to whoever needs to receive it. It is a formal letter of complaint about Detective Sergeant Birch. I have been harassed for the past couple of months and now my name has been given to the newspapers without a shred of evidence. This will result in me getting no work and I won't put up with it.'

The officer took the letter. Looking at Jimmy, he said: 'I promise you son, I will give it in, but don't hold your breath waiting for an answer. There's a double murder investigation going on and things have to be investigated.'

Jimmy turned and walked out of the station without bothering to say anymore. He made the return trip to his flat without speaking to a soul.

CHAPTER SEVENTEEN

Things continued much as they had before for Jimmy, except that the newspaper article had made people very wary of him. When he went in the shops, no-one spoke to him and some of the local kids would try to torment him by shouting 'killer' from a safe distance. Jimmy spent most of his time fishing; he knew he was being watched periodically by Detective Sergeant Birch but tried to ignore it. He hadn't heard anything back from his letter, but he wasn't surprised. To make his temper even worse, he still wasn't able to shake off his aches and pains.

In the town, a new manager had started at the bank and, each day at the same time, he went out into the park to eat his lunch. He was found murdered in the same way as the previous victim. Detective Sergeant Birch went straight down to the canal to look for Jimmy but he was nowhere to be found. A constable was placed outside his flat to wait for him to return. It was two days before Jimmy showed up. He was immediately arrested and taken to the station. Once again, he faced the detective and was questioned.

'Okay, where have you been this time?'

'In the peak district, hiking. I'm fed up with people treating me like a leper and wanted to get away for a while.'

The detective looked at him in disbelief: 'I don't suppose you can prove it.'

'As a matter of fact, I can. Yesterday I filled up my water bottle at a farmhouse and spent some time talking to the farmer.'

'And the day before?'

'From early that morning, I set out on public transport to get up to the peaks. So, no, I have no alibi unless someone can remember me,' replied Jimmy.

He was beginning to feel irritated by the whole thing; he just wanted to get on with his life.

When he was asked the location of the farmhouse, he easily pointed it out on the map. The police immediately checked out Jimmy's story and the farmer confirmed that he had been at the farmhouse.

'That doesn't let you off; there is still a chance you killed the victim.'

'Oh yeah, and got back here after going all that way, just to get water from a farmer, and then travelled back on public transport. You've got to be joking' said Jimmy.

'We are awaiting a report from the pathologist on the exact time of death and, until we get it, you're staying here.'

Turning toward the uniformed policeman in the corner of the room, he said: 'Keep an eye on him; I'm going out for a bit.'

With that, the detective left the room. Jimmy put his head in his hands in disbelief. Why was this happening to him? About half an hour later, he was told he could go. After sitting so long in one place, he was stiff. His

Point the Finger of Blame

hip ached as he stood up; after a quick stretch, Jimmy spoke to the constable, demanding to see the superintendent. He was surprised when the superintendent met with him. Jimmy told him that what was happening was nothing short of harassment; he felt that Detective Sergeant Birch had a personal vendetta against him and that he was allowing his personal judgement to cloud the investigation. Jimmy said he would see a solicitor about pressing charges if it continued. The superintendent said he would look into the matter and get back to him with a progress report within twenty four hours. With this, Jimmy left the police station and made his way home once more.

The post mortem report threw up several puzzles. At first, the pathologist had suspected that the man had been shot, due to both an entry and exit wound. But, he concluded that a skewer type implement had been pushed right though the eye socket and into the brain. Slight traces of water and gold had been found in the wound. The estimated time of death had indicated that, on balance, Jimmy could not have been involved.

The next day, well within the twenty four hours, there was a knock on the flat door. When Jimmy opened it, he was surprised to see the superintendent standing there.

'Hello Mr McLeod. I'm sorry to bother you but I felt it was best I came to speak to you, person to person. I have looked at your case. I feel that your belief that you are being harassed may have some merit. As you know, there is a full scale murder hunt in progress at the moment and it is difficult for my men at this time. More people are being killed, even as we try to find the killer. I am not justifying any behaviour but I do understand, probably better than you, the pressures this puts on the person involved. I have decided to remove Detective Sergeant Birch from the case and appoint Detective Friar; he has more experience in this type of investigation. From this point, I will also be overseeing this case myself. I hope this is sufficient to allay any fears you may have. I cannot say that you will not be interviewed in the future, however, as you do remain a suspect.'

Jimmy listened to what the superintendent had to say without interruption; he had the feeling that the superintendent was sizing him up as he was speaking. It reminded Jimmy of some of the army officers from his past.

'Thank you for coming yourself. I am innocent and, after your men have caught the person responsible, I will expect a full apology printed in the papers. I am not a vindictive man but I need to have my reputation restored. It's hard enough getting work as it is, without this sort of thing hanging over my head.'

He could tell that the superintendent was only visiting because he felt he had to and not because he thought Jimmy was innocent. But, at least it was a start.

After the superintendent had left, Jimmy decided to go fishing; he needed some time to think and found fishing the time when he could best relax. The older he was getting, the more he found that being outside, with only himself for company, was when he enjoyed life the most. He had a good day and caught several fish but, instead of staying at the canal overnight as he intended, he went home and slept in his bed. He still hadn't managed to shake off his aches and pains and didn't fancy sleeping on the hard ground.

Point the Finger of Blame

The next morning he was back at the canal; he spent the day without seeing another soul. It was midweek. None of the normal dog walkers were about and Colin was at school. On his way back from the canal later that afternoon, he went into the corner shop to buy his normal paper. The shopkeeper actually said hello. It wasn't until he sat down to read the paper that he found out why. Detective Friar had arranged a twenty-four-hour a day stake out at the park and, after two days, they had arrested a local handyman on suspicion of murdering the bank manager. It seemed the police had seen a man walking around in the park with a bucket in his hand. Something caused the police to become suspicious and they stopped and searched him. In the bucket they found a slender file with its handle wrapped in chamois leather. There was also a short handled trowel.

After questioning, it appeared the man couldn't account for his movements at the time of the murder. He said that, due the nature of his work, he was always moving about from one small job to another. The tools in the bucket had caused the police to be suspicions as they appeared to fit the description of a likely weapon. He said the file was one he used to sharpen people's knives. After forensic examination, the file was found to have minute traces of gold and blood of the same match as the victim. The bucket had some water in the bottom, so this would account for both the gold and water in the wound.

The man, whose name was George Bennett, was asked about the traces of gold and, after much thought, he said that he had done quite a bit of work for a widow, Mrs Nott, who lives in the town. She had been getting some coal in and had snagged her wedding ring. She asked him to make it smoother as she kept catching her cloths on the snag. He had used the file to smooth it down.

The police went to check the story. On arrival, the policeman knocked on the door and, briefly showing his warrant card, he went on to ask her if she had recently damaged her wedding ring.

Before he got chance to say more, she shouted at him: 'I haven't got a ring, so you won't be able to steal it. Get off with you or I will call the police!'

With that, she grabbed a broom which stood by the door and started to hit him, shouting at the top of her voice for help as she did so.

A neighbour came running round the corner and, recognising the policeman, managed to calm Mrs Nott down. Once again, the policeman showed his warrant card. The neighbour explained that Mrs Nott was very confused and had been getting worse over the recent months. The policeman calmed the old lady down and returned to the station to report what had happened. He had noted, however, that she had not been wearing a ring. Together with the other findings, it was decided that they had enough evidence to charge George Bennett with murder.

Jimmy gave a sigh of relief and relaxed for the first time since this whole nightmare had started. He hadn't realised how it had affected him till now. In many ways, he felt like he had when returning from one of his missions in Korea. He soon fell asleep. When he woke he felt stiff all over; every joint in his back and legs seemed to ache. He thought he must have slept awkwardly so stood up and stretched, then moved

Point the Finger of Blame

around the flat in an effort to loosen his muscles. He figured that he had been getting a bit stressed with all the police attention and, now that was sorted, he would soon return to normal.

The trial of George Bennett started three weeks later, with so much evidence that there didn't seem any reason to delay. Jimmy bought a paper every day and followed the trial with great interest. He wasn't going fishing much as he found walking and sitting on the canal bank painful to his hip joints. Over the next few weeks, he couldn't seem to get rid of the stiffness. He had a swelling over his right hip which he put down to walking with a limp; he took aspirin, which seemed to help a bit, but didn't feel like getting around much. The best he could manage was to walk to the shops and back for his paper and groceries. The evidence presented at court made for fascinating reading. He read with interest about blood found on the file; it was confirmed to be the same group as that of the bank manager. The defence did point out that the blood also matched that of the accused but it didn't help his case. The police never found the ring from Mrs Nott's house, despite a complete search of her house and garden; so, it was assumed stolen by George Bennett. With lack of proof, however, this charge was never pressed. No evidence was found that directly connected the first murder with George Bennett. However, the fact that the method of killing had been very similar felt like enough to convict George of both murders. The trial was a short one. George Bennett was found guilty of murder and given a life sentence, with a minimum of 21 years.

After the case had finished, the park was once more used freely by the locals. The drunken behaviour of the students again became a problem. Although Jimmy went through the park to the shops, he never stopped. The damage the students were causing upset him and he watched all his hard work go to waste. The council had grassed over all the flower beds to help reduce the vandalism. Over the following weeks, Jimmy felt more and more unwell. Neither the pain in his joints or the swelling settled, so he eventually made an appointment to see his doctor. Dr Brown was surprised to see him.

'In all the time you've been my patient, this is the first time you've come to the surgery. What can I do for you?'

Jimmy explained what had happened and how long the pain had been going on for. After giving Jimmy a full examination, the doctor looked at him.

'I'm not sure what is happening but I think we had best get you checked out properly. I will arrange for some x-rays to be taken.'

The doctor picked up the phone and arranged for him to go to the district hospital in the morning.

'On your way out, make another appointment for the end of the week; I should have the results by then. I have prescribed some stronger painkillers for you. Let me know if things get any worse before I see you next.'

With that, Jimmy went out of the room and collected his prescription. He made another appointment and slowly walked home. By the time he got back he was in agony, so he took some painkillers and went to bed.

The next morning, he made his way to the district hospital where he had his x-rays. While he was there, he was sent down to the accident and emergency department to collect some crutches. With that, he went home. At the end of the week, he went back to the

Point the Finger of Blame

doctor's surgery and saw Dr Brown once more. Dr Brown said he would need to take a blood sample and that a specialist at the hospital wanted to see him that afternoon. When Jimmy asked what was wrong with him, Dr Brown looked at him for a moment.

'Well, Mr McLeod, we aren't a hundred percent certain at the moment, which is why I need to take a blood sample and why the specialist wants to see you. But, it may be bad news I'm afraid.'

He paused and looked at Jimmy once more, as if trying to gauge what his reaction would be.

'Look Doctor, I realise you aren't sure but I'd rather have some idea of what I might be facing. I've been in pain for some time now, so if you have any ideas I want to know them.'

'Alright, I suppose you need to know.' Dr Brown took a deep breath. 'The symptoms and x-rays combined suggest that there may be a possibility you have bone cancer. As I said, we need to do further tests to be sure; the man I'm sending you to is one of the best. We are lucky to have him at the district hospital. He has asked to see you this afternoon.'

Dr Brown looked at Jimmy, trying to gauge his reaction to the news. But he could tell nothing by what he was seeing.

'Okay Doctor, well let's get things sorted. What time shall I go up to the hospital and where do I go?'

Doctor Brown explained what Jimmy needed to do and arranged to see him again in three days time.

Jimmy left the surgery, deep in thought. He hadn't expected such bad news but nothing could be done until he knew the results of all the tests. He caught the bus home and waited until it was time to make his way up to the hospital.

CHAPTER EIGHTEEN

Jimmy gave himself plenty of time to get to the hospital in case he needed to stop on the way. Even with the crutches and painkillers he was finding every movement painful. Once there he found his way to the correct department, after going through a maze of corridors. It was an old hospital and had bits added on over the years, so it had become very spread out. After checking in at the department, he was sent off for more blood tests and x-rays. After these had been done, he made his way back to the waiting room. By now he was in a great deal of pain. The x-ray and phlebotomy departments were some way away from each other and he had walked farther than he would have normally. He was soon called into the consultant's room.

'Good afternoon, Mr McLeod. Please take a seat. My name is Dr Scott. I have looked at your previous x-rays and blood tests and also the x-rays you've just had taken. Now, could you please tell me when the pain and swelling began?'

Jimmy answered all of the consultant's questions and then was given a tougher examination. After that, he sat down, exhausted.

DEREK SMITH

'Well Mr McLeod, I'm afraid the news does not appear to be too good. Do you have any close family or friends you would like with you as I explain?'

Jimmy explained that he lived alone; all his family were in Scotland and he hadn't seen them for several years.

'Don't worry Doc. I can take what you need to say, just tell me straight.'

'I think you have probably already guessed that the news is not good. You have cancer of the bone. I suspect you have had it for some time. It has spread quickly and there is little we can do for you, except manage the pain. I'm afraid you probably have only a short time left; it won't be long before you will need inpatient care to control the pain. I suggest you contact your parents.'

Dr Scott looked at Jimmy all the time he spoke. He noticed Jimmy's sharp intake of breath as he was told he would die soon. But, otherwise he saw no sign of emotion.

'I'm sorry Mr McLeod. I wish it were better news but this type of cancer can be very aggressive; at this time we have very little we can offer you, except pain control.'

'Don't worry about me Sir, I can cope. I thought it might be something nasty once I had seen Dr Brown, so it wasn't a total surprise.'

Jimmy spent some time talking through things with the consultant and arranged to see him again.

'I will phone your GP and get him to come out to your home tomorrow so we can start sorting things out for you.'

With that, Jimmy set off home. He had a lot to think about, not least whether to write to his parents. It was such a long time since he'd written, it would be hard to write with such bad news. He could phone the Laird and ask to speak to his father. However, he didn't even know if the Laird was still in charge of the estate or whether Jonathan had taken over.

Although he had already been told by Dr Brown, it was still a shock to have it confirmed; a part of him had still hoped a mistake had been made. He got off the bus one stop early to walk through the park. It was hard going but he wanted to see something near to the wild places he knew as a child; unfortunately, this was the nearest he could get to that. He sat at the bench where he used to feed the squirrel and hardly noticed as one came out from the bushes. But, then, it jumped onto the seat beside him.

'Sorry mate, I've got nothing for you.'

Then he remembered he had a packet of nuts and raisins in his pocket. He'd bought them to take to the hospital as he had thought he would be a long time. He sat and fed the squirrel; it was almost as if the animal understood that he needed that contact with wildlife. He thought he was being daft but he felt as if the animal had come to say goodbye to him. He sat there, enjoying those precious moments with nature, knowing they might be the last chance he would have to be with wildlife. For the first time in his life, he felt lonely. He wished his parents were closer. He felt as if he'd let them down somehow. Jimmy decided there and then that he wouldn't contact them. He didn't think it would be fair to worry them, as there wasn't anything they could do, so it would be better for them not to know until afterwards. He would leave a letter. With that, the squirrel jumped down and ran into the bushes and up the nearby tree.

Jimmy went home and tried to rest. He knew in his heart that he didn't have much time left; probably less than the couple of months the consultant had suggested. Jimmy was a realist, if nothing else. He kicked himself for not going to the doctor earlier, but then, it might not have made any difference; as the consultant had told him, there was little that could be done.

The next morning his general practitioner called round to the flat.

'I'm really sorry Mr McLeod, I have spoken to the hospital. Is there anything I can do to help you at all? Would you like me to arrange for your parents to be able to come and be with you at this time?'

Jimmy handed the doctor an envelope.

'I don't want them to know before, nothing will be gained by that; but, can you post this when I'm gone? It's a letter for my parents.'

'Of course.'

The doctor then asked him whether he thought he could cope on his own in the flat. Jimmy thought about it and said he was finding it increasingly difficult to cope. After a discussion, the doctor told him that there was a bed for him at the hospice. He would take him there later on that afternoon if Jimmy felt he wanted to go.

'You may find that, after they've sorted out your pain control, you will be able to cope back here with help. I think in the meantime you would be wise to have the help they can give you. I checked before I came out and they do have a bed, if you want to go in this afternoon.'

Point the Finger of Blame

Jimmy thought about it for a short while and agreed it made sense to have the help.

'It's for the best. They can look after you and help with the pain. I don't think you are coping well here and you need some help. It's not like a hospital ward. Gather together what you want to take with you and I will pick you up in a couple of hours.'

With that, he left Jimmy to sort things out. He collected together a few clothes and realised, for the first time, how little he owned. At least who ever cleaned out the flat wouldn't have much to do. He didn't even have any photos of his family and again found himself wishing he had kept in touch with his parents. There never seemed much time and he had moved about so much. It was too late now to wish for what might have been.

Later that afternoon, the doctor returned and helped Jimmy to put his belongings in the car. Off they went. Jimmy was surprised at the hospice; he hadn't realised that there were such places. He was lucky; evidently there weren't many of them around yet. Most terminal patients were still treated in general wards. The hospice was set in beautiful countryside. On arrival, he was met by a nurse who introduced herself as Aida. She was about twenty five years old with a slim figure and long black hair. Jimmy noticed her smile and wondered how she could be happy working in a place where people came to die.

Aida showed him to his room. He had a view of the countryside from his window; not a house in sight. Jimmy noticed a few shrubs with berries to one side; it was full of birds making the most of the easy food. He had a room to himself. Although it wasn't big, it was comfortable, and he didn't have many belongs to find homes for. Aida explained the various rules and procedures and then went to get him a cup of tea. When she came back, Aida told him he could have visitors whenever he liked. He explained that he would have no visitors as no one knew he was here. He wanted it that way. She didn't press him but looked sad that he was alone at such a time. They sat down and Aida asked him all sorts of questions, carefully writing down the answers.

By the time they had finished, Jimmy was tired, so Aida left him to rest. He sat and looked around his small room. So this is where I'm going to spend my last days, he thought. He wished he was back in Oban, up on the hills watching the deer and hawks, but it wasn't to be. After about an hour, there was a gentle knock on the door. A different nurse had brought him his supper. He looked down at it. A baked potato, fish and peas, with stewed apple and custard for pudding; at least he would be eating better than he had lately in the flat. Since he had been unwell, he had not bothered to cook for himself so he had been eating quick snacks. It had been some time since he had enjoyed a meal. Perhaps it wouldn't be so bad. After he had eaten, he decided to go to bed early. He found the toilet across the corridor and, on his way back to his room, he met a man in a wheelchair.

'Hello, I'm Jimmy.' He held out his hand.

'Bugger off,' came the grumpy reply.

Jimmy didn't mind. He figured that if you'd come here to die, you had a right to be bad tempered. Then he went back, had a wash, and went to bed. He couldn't sleep, although he was exhausted; he heard a quiet tap on the door.

Point the Finger of Blame

'Come in.'

Aida entered.

'You're in bed early. I have brought you some pain killers; they will help you settle. If you need anyone in the night, ring your bell. If you can't sleep and want to talk or have a cup of tea, just let us know.'

She left as quietly as she had come, seeming to understand that he didn't want to talk.

Jimmy laid awake, thinking of the past. He thought of when he was a child up in the mountains with his father and how, as soon as they got home, his mum would have a hot drink for them. He remembered the big house and the Laird and his family; how he had thought he would live there forever. He would have liked that. Jimmy again regretted not keeping in touch with his parents; he had been so angry at how he'd had to leave that he just never seemed to find the right time to write. He wondered how his parents were and what they were doing. He hoped they were happy.

His mind drifted to the war years and the killing he had done. Had he been right to become a sniper? All that time alone had reinforced his preference for his own company. It felt right at the time. Jimmy gradually fell into an exhausted sleep, helped by the tablets.

CHAPTER NINETEEN

Next morning, he woke early and got himself washed and dressed. He remembered Aida had said that breakfast was at eight o'clock. There was a dining room if he felt like company or if he rang his bell, someone would bring it to him in his room. He decided he would save them the fuss and walked down the corridor, following the sound of rattling cups. It seemed a long walk and he was glad of his crutches. He was met by one of the staff members who asked him what he wanted. He was obviously early as he had the place to himself so, after he had his breakfast, he went back to his room. Aida was just about to knock on his door.

'I'm here. I've just been down for breakfast, have you been working all night?'
"No, I was on a late shift yesterday and an early today. I've just brought you your pain killers. Did you have a good night?'

'Not too bad, considering it was only the day before yesterday that I was told I was dying, and now I find myself here.'

Point the Finger of Blame

'I'm sorry, I didn't realise you had only just found out. It must have been a heck of a shock. How have you been managing at home?'

'Lousy. The past months have been hell. I should have realised earlier, I suppose, but so much has happened in the past months that it just seemed to follow on. I hate doctors, so I thought I could sort myself out.'

Aida followed him into the room and sat with him as he cried for the first time. It had finally sunk in that he was dying and there was nothing he could do about it. After a while he calmed down and looked at Aida.

'Sorry to be such a baby. I haven't sobbed since I was a little 'un.'

'Do you want to be left alone for a while?'

'Yes please.'

'I'll come back in a while. Ring if you want me, won't you?'

Jimmy nodded and she left the room. He supposed she was used to dealing with such things; she seemed to know that he needed space.

The next few weeks seemed to drift past Jimmy; the pain got worse and worse and he was taking more painkillers each day. He found himself spending more and more time in bed. When he was awake, he would sit by the window in a comfortable chair they had provided him with. He started to mull over things in his mind. Time and time again, he found himself deeply regretting not keeping in contact with his parents. It was too late now. The nurses had asked him if they could contact them but he refused. Too much water had passed under the bridge. He wasn't going to get them worried now it was too late. He thought about the times he had spent on his own in the Korean jungle and whether things would have been different if he hadn't become a sniper; was this his punishment for killing? Why did he get in that fight with Jonathan? Without that, that he might have been a gamekeeper now and been living in the wild places he loved. If he closed his eyes and concentrated, he could still picture the Scottish landscape that he so loved. There were many things he'd done in his life that couldn't be changed but there was something he could sort out. It wouldn't change the past but it might just help someone else's future. After thinking it through, he rang and asked Aida if she could contact the police station and leave a message for Detective Birch, asking to see him. She looked at Jimmy with a frown on her face.

'I'm going home early today as I have some time owing me. I go past the police station so I will pop in for you rather than phone. Do you want me to take a note?'

'No, just tell him I want to speak to him. He will remember me, don't worry.'

Aida didn't ask any more but promised to call in.

It was two days later before Jimmy heard anything. Just after supper, Jimmy had lain down on his bed and a knock on the door woke him from a snooze. A nurse opened the door.

'You've got a visitor Jimmy. Is it okay if he comes in?'

Before he had time to answer, Detective Birch walked in past the nurse and held out his hand. Taking Jimmy's hand he gave it a gentle shake. Detective Birch was surprised at the sight of Jimmy; he appeared to have aged considerably in the last couple of years.

Point the Finger of Blame

'I got your message, Mr McLeod. Nice to see you again. I was sorry to hear you were at the hospice.'

'Thank you, for I'm in no fit state to visit you I'm afraid.'

Gesturing for the detective to sit down, Jimmy took a deep breath and said: 'I asked you here to confess to the murders in the park.'

Jimmy heard the detective take a sharp intake of breath.

'Are you doing this to get the other guy off the hook? He's been found guilty and you need to explain a bit more. You need to be able to prove that you are the killer.'

'I realise that. I'm doing this to put right a wrong. The wrong man is in jail. I stood by and let him take the rap for something I did. I always felt that you knew the wrong man was blamed but you couldn't prove it, so now I'll tell you the whole story.'

'I need to get a witness to this and I also need to read you your rights.'

'I know my rights and, don't worry, I won't change my mind. So just listen.'

With that there was a tap on the door. Aida entered.

'I have just come to give you your painkillers Jimmy. I heard you had a visitor; do you both want a cup of tea? The trolley's outside.'

Jimmy took the tablets; he was in pain and he wanted a clear head.

'Thanks for the offer. Can you leave us both a cup, we've got a lot of talking to do.'

With that, Aida asked the girl outside to leave two cups. Realising that now was not the time to ask who

Jimmy's visitor was, she left the room with her usual "call if you need anything."

The two men looked at each other, waiting for the other to speak.

'I will tell you the whole story but I'm not going to have someone else sitting here. What you guys missed was that it wasn't a blunt instrument that killed the men, it was a .22 bullet.'

The detective butted in.

'If it had been a bullet, it would have gone straight through the skull or lodged in the skull; either way, we would have found the bullet. You're going to have to do better than that.'

'What if I told you that the bullet was made of ice and melted in no time with the body heat?'

'Rubbish. You can't shoot an ice bullet - it would shatter.'

'What makes you think that? Get your note pad and pencil out and I'll tell you how it was done.'

But Jimmy found himself beginning to get sleepy; the painkillers where taking effect sooner than he had counted on.

'I'm sorry; you'll have to come back tomorrow morning. I'll tell you everything then but come alone.'

Detective Birch gave a shrug. Before he had time to reply, Jimmy was asleep.

CHAPTER TWENTY

Detective Birch arrived back at the hospice just after Jimmy had eaten his breakfast.
Wasting no time, he asked Jimmy if he still wanted to persist in his story.

'It's no story, as you will discover. Look, I can't keep calling you Detective Birch; it's too much of a mouthful. What's your first name?'

'William, but you can call me Bill, if you like.'

Jimmy smiled. The thought of a policeman being called Bill was ironic.

'You were born to work for the Old Bill then.'

The detective had heard that joke so many times; it didn't worry him anymore, so he ignored Jimmy's remark.

'Take a seat and I'll get a move on. I get so tired now and I want to tell you as much as possible. I know I haven't got much time left.'

Bill sat down on the chair opposite Jimmy. It seemed strange looking out at such a beautiful view and talking about murder.

'Just listen and ask questions later.'
Bill nodded.

DEREK SMITH

'I was brought up in Scotland, the son of a gillie - that's a gamekeeper to you. I thought I'd follow in my dad's footsteps and then I got called up for my national service, just as Korea was kicking off. To cut a long story short, I was selected to be a sniper and was given all the training and left to get on with it. I was good, very good. I killed lots of men for King and country. After the war, I was sent home, just like that. They'd made me a lone killer and didn't care what happened after.'

Jimmy winced in pain; the memories weren't good ones.

'I had been trained as a killing machine and that's what I did for three years, without questioning my orders. Then, after all, the war finished in stalemate, with neither side winning. But hundreds of thousands of people were killed or maimed losing arms and legs. Some lost their minds, including women and kids, and for what? The soldiers came home from war to nothing.'

Jimmy paused, as if remembering that time. He shuddered, and then continued.

'We came home to a country run by powerful people who don't care about anyone but themselves; they didn't care about anyone less fortunate. After I got home, I couldn't settle down and I got into a fight with the Laird's nephew. I was taken to court and then told to leave the estate. So, I had to leave my family and all I had known for a second time. I've never been back since. I was given a job on a building site and made friends; my life was coming together. Then, I got into another fight protecting a mate from a bully. I ended up in jail for three months; fought the wrong man again. Daddy had influence. I lost everything, again. The social worker sorted out a flat and a job for me when I left prison. Even then, I kept being pushed around. I even lost my job there because of jumped up little pratts who thought they were better than everyone else; just cause their dads were rich. Well, I finally had enough. It was when the student killed a poor defenceless squirrel for fun, just because I was feeding it.'

Jimmy paused, a tear collecting in the corner of his eye at the thought of the squirrel's body lying bloodied and twisted on the ground.

'I had always had guns, right from a lad. When I left the estate in Scotland, I brought my gun with me; it had been a present from my father. I had kept it hidden away in a bit of tube, wrapped in some grease cloth, and mixed in with my fishing kit. A mate looked after my stuff when I was inside. He didn't even know the gun was there. So, after a lot of thought, I decided to wage my own war and kill off some of the bastards to make the world a better place. It was easy; after all, the army had trained me to kill and not get caught.'

Jimmy fell silent. Bill sat quietly as if not wanting to interrupt.

'I wanted to show them that their money wouldn't save them. I wouldn't be kicked about anymore just because they had money and I didn't. I could kill them and they wouldn't be able to stop me; my gun made me more powerful than any of them. So, I set out to commit the perfect murder and, if it wasn't for the cancer, I could have carried on killing for years.'

Jimmy reached over and picked up his glass of water. Taking a sip, he started talking again. It was as if a tap had been turned on; he needed to explain what had happened before he died. Despite the growing pain, he wanted to keep talking, so he didn't call for more painkillers. He knew they would make him sleepy and he had so much to tell.

'I had been thinking for some time of a way of shooting someone without trace. I made my first ice bullets and took them with me in a flask when I went to the canal, fishing. I found a remote spot, set up a target, and fired the ice bullets; but, the heat generated from them rushed down the barrel and distorted the shape so they didn't fire true. They wouldn't be accurate enough. So, back to the drawing board. I tried everything until at last I found that, if I covered the ice with a layer of gold leaf, I could keep the bullet from melting as it travelled down the barrel. The gold leaf mostly burnt away but it was enough to keep accuracy.

'I then had to find a way of concealing the gun and the small amount of ammunition I had so it wouldn't be found either on me or in the flat.'

Jimmy's voice was becoming more and more slurred and his eyes kept shutting. By the time he had finished his last sentence, he had fallen asleep. Bill sat looking at Jimmy for a few minutes in case he woke again. He glanced down at his watch and was surprised to see he had been with Jimmy for over two hours. Then, he quietly got up and left the room. Bill found it difficult to believe he was telling the truth but, at the same time, he couldn't see a reason for him to be making it up. He hadn't known that Jimmy had been a sniper and wondered if doing something like that could turn a man's mind. Jimmy certainly seemed to feel he had been let down. Bill could see how it would be difficult to return back to normality after such a way of life. He hadn't thought about that sort of thing before but he couldn't understand why such people weren't given

Point the Finger of Blame

more support once their services were no longer required. How could you just come back and pick up the threads of your life after killing people in such a cold blooded fashion? It certainly gave him something to think about.

Bill wrote up his notes from the morning's conversation with Jimmy. Then, he got on the telephone to trace Jimmy's army career. It took him much longer than he thought. It seemed that sniper's records were not readably available and it took him several hours to track down what he needed. Although he wasn't allowed detailed information, he was able to confirm that Jimmy had indeed been a sniper in Korea. The army wasn't able to tell him what had happened to Jimmy after discharge as it did not keep such information.

Well, it appeared that he was telling the truth about both his army career and the fact that, once he'd left the forces after Korea, the army had no further part in his life. Bill found this surprising; he thought that they would have kept a bit of an eye on personnel who had been involved in such specialised areas. Bill then checked on the police records at Oban. He found reference to Jimmy's arrest following his fight with the Laird's nephew and the resulting suspended sentence. With the Laird being involved, it seemed obvious that Jimmy would have been asked to leave the area. The records of his later prison sentence were easily available. It seemed he had behaved himself in prison. It all seemed to follow the story that Jimmy had told him.

By the time he had followed up the details, it was time for him to knock off for the day. So, he went home, determined to get more done in the morning. Bill decided to go straight to see Jimmy first thing in the morning. He hoped that, by going early, Jimmy might be able to talk longer before getting tired. He popped into his local corner shop and bought some fruit to take with him. Afterwards, he wondered what he was thinking of taking fruit to a man who was confessing to two murders. It was strange; he felt sorry for Jimmy. He had done a dirty job for his country in a time of war, yet they had discarded him when he was no longer needed. Bill couldn't help but wonder if things would have been different if Jimmy had been given some support before his return to civilian life.

The nurses let him straight in when he arrived at the hospice. Jimmy was being helped into his chair when he entered the room. It was obvious to Bill that Jimmy was getting weaker all the time. The nurses looked up.

'We've just finished and we will leave you two in peace.'

Turning once more to Jimmy, one of them said: 'don't forget to give us a call if you want anything.'

Jimmy nodded, but didn't say anything.

'We will leave you in peace with your friend.'

They both left the room and shut the door behind them.

'I haven't told the staff anything. They might not want to look after a murderer, after all.'

He looked up at Bill, as if expecting an argument.

'They won't get anything from me at the moment Jimmy. As far as they know I'm just a visitor, until I've gathered all the evidence. As you are well aware, the case has been officially closed.'

Jimmy nodded and gestured at Bill to sit down.

'I can't keep looking up, so sit down.'

Point the Finger of Blame

Bill sat down and put the fruit on the side, without saying anything.

'Let's get on with it then,' said Jimmy. 'I don't have time to waste.'

'Before you start, can you tell me how you concealed the gun and bullets? We went through your place with a fine-tooth comb.'

Jimmy smiled.

'You looked in the wrong place. I'm not daft; I told you I had been planning this for some time. When I worked in the park, making the flower beds, I came across drainage pipes just under the turf. They should have been deeper but they weren't. Then, I found a manhole just in the bushes; over time, the leaves and soil had covered it over. I hit it with my spade when I was gardening. It was just right, hidden from view by the bushes. I lifted the cover and it was obvious that this part of the drainage was no longer in use; probably disused since the old houses had been demolished and the new estate built. It was a real stroke of luck. The drain pipes weren't deep and it was as dry as a bone. I wrapped my gun up to keep it clean and slid it into the manhole, carefully replacing the soil and leaves. The bullets, don't forget, were made of ice. Once made, I put them in the ice box, in a packet of fish fingers, and carefully resealed it. Even if anyone had found them, it was highly unlikely they would have seen them as anything other than an ice collection. I didn't put the gold leaf on them until I needed them.'

Jimmy stopped for a minute or two, as if gathering the strength to go on.

'My biggest problem was getting the gold leaf to stay on. I had to keep them really cold and get them down to the gun in the park. I found a small piece of tubing just the right size and then made them up in lolly moulds that kept them frozen. All I had to do was break the ice-lolly and get the tube out. All I needed to do then was load the gun and fire. I couldn't waste any time or the bullet would begin to melt. I only had one bullet at a time so I couldn't miss. Not much chance of that happening.'

Again, Jimmy paused. Bill was amazed at what he was hearing.

'I was lucky. The first person to come along was the student that had caused me so much grief. I knew he was the one that killed the squirrel I had been feeding. It couldn't have worked out better. I had been lying in the bushes with the gun when he arrived alone; he was waiting for the others. I couldn't miss; he was only thirty yards away. I quickly loaded the gun, took careful aim, and fired. As long as the bullet held its shape for long enough, I knew he would be dead as soon as the bullet left the gun. I quickly put the gun into its hiding place beside me and replaced the manhole, making sure to cover it back up with the leaves and soil. I quickly looked to make sure I had left no trace. In the moments it took me to hide it, his mates had arrived and found him. One of them went to call the police. There was a dense conifer tree beside the bushes and I quickly climbed high up into its cover and lay still in the branches. It was like being back in Korea. The police combed the area for hours with no luck. They closed the park off and left a couple of bobbies on the gate. I stayed dead still up in the tree until the early hours and then made my escape and went off to the canal; I had the army to thank for my ability to cover miles quickly over country. I'd hidden my fishing gear up a tree by the canal a couple of days before; I quickly retrieved it and set up, as if I'd been fishing all night.'

Jimmy stopped for a few moments. He was getting tired.

'I was sat there when the police arrived. It had worked even better than expected. The bullet had gone though the eye socket as planned but didn't go though the back of the skull, leaving the bullet to quickly melt in the remaining body heat. A .22 bullet is small and doesn't leave a trace. The gold was completely removed on the bullet leaving the gun. I found slight traces when I cleaned the gun later.'

Jimmy was staring out of the window. They both sat in silence; Bill was amazed at what Jimmy had done and at the quiet and calm way he told his story. It was obvious to the detective that he felt no remorse. He'd just done what he felt needed doing. After a few moments, he turned to Bill.

'I need to rest, but can you come back later this afternoon?'

Bill agreed and left, asking the nurse to go and see Jimmy, as he went.

Bill went to the nearest cafe and ordered a tea and sandwiches. He needed to think and the police station wasn't the place to get peace. He found it strange that, even whilst Jimmy had been telling him what he had done, he didn't feel any repugnance at the information he was being given. He put it down to the way Jimmy presented the facts; just as if he was reporting to a senior officer. The only time he showed any emotion was when he talked about the student killing the squirrel. It was as if Jimmy looked on the murder as a continuation of his actions in Korea. But then, Bill supposed that Jimmy would have had to justify the manner in which he killed the Koreans, otherwise he wouldn't have been able to do King and country.

Bill went back to the station and, after speaking to the superintendent, took another detective and one of the forensic team down to the park. He found the manhole and gun, well wrapped and oiled for protection, just as Jimmy had described. The area was once more cordoned off. He left the forensic expert with the other detective and made his way back to the hospice.

Jimmy was in bed when he entered the room. He was looking very frail but Bill couldn't spare the time to let him sleep. It was obvious to him that Jimmy didn't have much time left and he needed to get the rest of the story. At present, Jimmy had only discussed the student's murder. It had been the bank manager's murder that George Bennett had been put in prison for, even though, due to the similar ways each the two men had died, it had been assumed that he had killed both men. If Bill was to get George out of prison, he needed the whole story.

Jimmy opened his eyes. 'I'm glad you're back. Sit down and I will continue my story.'

Bill sat down once more and waited for him to speak.

'I suppose you want to know what happened with the next guy.'

Bill nodded.

'Well, after the fuss had died down a bit, I decided to see if I could repeat the exercise. I went down to the park on a couple of occasions but, each time, there

Point the Finger of Blame

were too many people about. The only real chance I had was with a young woman but she had a small child with her, so I let her go. Anyway, I had no argument with women and kids. I started to watch the park and look for patterns. I noticed that the manager from the local bank had started to go down to the park at lunchtime. He always went to the quieter area of the park. I had heard he was making life difficult for some of the locals since he had taken over. He had called in several overdrafts, so he had lots of people who didn't like him. He was obviously someone who used his position to make life hard for ordinary folks. The fact that he wasn't liked would make any investigation into his killing more difficult.

So, one lunch time, I set off with my ice bullet and made my way to the park. By getting in the shrubbery, I could get a good shot at him whilst he was having his lunch. He didn't stand a chance. Again, I quickly hid the gun and this time made my escape straight away. I had made my plans carefully and had worked out how far I could get before the police could find me. I made sure that, as soon as I got in the area, I called on a farmhouse to ask for water, getting into conversation about my stay. I needed someone who had seen me in the area and I made out I had been in the area overnight. I knew that most people would always be vague about times when questioned later, so it would be difficult to prove I hadn't been there for longer than I had.

The trace of gold and water they found in the bank manager's brain was unfortunate but your forensics messed that one up. I felt sorry for George Bennett at first but I didn't think they would find him guilty. I thought, once I'd killed again, the police would realise he wasn't their man. But then I found I was in too much pain and I knew I wouldn't be able to get enough distance between myself and the murder scene before the police caught up with me. So, I decided to wait until I felt better.'

He stopped once more and closed his eyes. Bill moved in his chair. Jimmy heard the movement and, thinking Bill was about to leave, he quickly spoke.

'Is there anything else you need to know?'

'Yes, what an earth gave you the idea to use ice bullets?'

Jimmy grinned.

'I saw a film where a marksman used ice bullets to kill his wife. I knew it wouldn't work, as they had said in the film, but it got me thinking. I started to experiment; I know guns inside out so it was just a case of trial and error.'

Bill still found it hard to believe that anyone could kill in such cold blood. Much as he felt sorry for Jimmy, he was also glad that he wouldn't be able to kill again. Bill was going through everything he had been told, trying to make sure he had all in information he needed.

'Get George Bennett out of prison won't you? I've done a lot in my life but I can at least put that right; as I said, if I hadn't got ill, I would have killed again and he would have been proved innocent. Could you do me a favour?'

Bill was caught off guard by this request. He hoped it was something he could do. He nodded.

'There's an insurance policy in my draw. Once the funeral is paid for, can you give the remainder to my parents? I would have loved to have seen them one more time. That's one thing I can't put right; I know what I have done will hurt them and I'm truly sorry for that. I would like my ashes scattered on the estate where I was born, up in the mountains. But you won't be able to do that. Oh, and give my fishing gear to young Colin who I used to fish with.'

With that, he closed his eyes. His breathing seemed easier, as if at last he had found some peace.

CHAPTER TWENTY-ONE

Bill went back to the station to see what was happening with the case. Jimmy's flat had been searched once more; the ice bullets had been found, just as he had said. They also found some gold leaf in one of the draws. The forensic team found a fingerprint on the inside of the manhole cover that matched the set they had taken from Jimmy at the time of his first arrest.

Now, the story was known. The evidence fully matched what they had been told and the processes were started to free George Bennett from prison. The next day, Bill went to the hospice to tell Jimmy that he was under arrest for murder. It was obvious to him that Jimmy would never stand trial; indeed, he would be moved straight to a prison hospital. As he went toward his room, he was stopped by a nurse.

'I'm sorry sir. I know you were a friend of Mr McLeod's. I'm afraid he died just after you left yesterday. We couldn't let you know as we didn't have your address. He asked us to give you this.' She handed him an insurance policy. 'He also said he had left a letter with his general practitioner for his parents and asked if you would take it to Scotland for him. It's

Point the Finger of Blame

strange he knew his time had come. This morning we found him dead in bed; he died peacefully in the night.'

Bill felt relieved that Jimmy had died; he hadn't looked forward to getting him moved. He had, at least, made sure an innocent man had his name cleared before he died. Bill went back to the station and informed the superintendent of Jimmy's death. He then contacted the general practitioner before offering to tell Jimmy's parents and to get the letter delivered. When Bill phoned Jimmy's parents, they were obviously distraught; they hadn't heard anything from him since he had left Scotland and had been unable to contact him themselves, being unable to trace him. Bill arranged for them to come to the funeral.

When Jimmy was cremated, there were only his parents, Aida from the hospice and Bill attending. The only other people there were the funeral directors. As they left the crematorium and stood outside, leaving their flowers, a squirrel jumped down out of a tree and sat watching the group for a few moments, before going on its way.

Bill took Brian and June to a pub for lunch afterwards and explained how he had become involved. By then, the story of George Bennett's wrongful imprisonment had hit the national headlines. Brian and June were very upset at what their son had done and how he had died. Bill was able to comfort them and explained that he felt Jimmy's experiences as a sniper in Korea had affected his mind. Bill explained how, in the end, Jimmy had confessed so that an innocent man did not stay in prison. He then gave the couple the letter Jimmy had left for them and said his goodbyes.

DEREK SMITH

Once he left, Jimmy's parents sat and talked well into the night and, next morning, they caught the train back to Scotland. They took his ashes with them, as well as the unopened letter. The following morning, Brian and June set off up the mountain path to Brian's favourite spot and scattered his ashes. At last, Jimmy had his wish; he was back home in his beloved mountains, amid the wildlife and beauty. Brian and June sat there for a moment or two before opening his letter. Jimmy had told his story since leaving home and apologised for not keeping in touch. He ended by saying how much he had missed them both and how he loved them. His last line was to ask forgiveness for what he was putting them through. The couple sat for several hours, quietly weeping for their only son and what could have been, before making their way slowly back home.

Author Profile

Derek Smith was born in a village on the edge of Salisbury Plain in 1945, the middle child of five whose father was a farm labourer. After attending the village school, Derek worked in the building trade from the age of fifteen until the end of his working life. He says he has always been a daydreamer with an active imagination and was told off on more than one occasion at school for this. During his working life Derek met many weird and wonderful characters and heard many stories from them, before being forced to retire after an accident at work in his 50s. Being a fan of western films, he had always wanted to write a cowboy book but was always too busy; he then seized the opportunity and, whilst walking his dogs, Derek started to daydream. He gradually developed stories and started to put them down on paper for his grandchildren to read after he was gone. His cowboy book is still a dream, but his present book was inspired from some of the men he worked with who fought in Korea.

Publisher Information

Rowanvale Books provides assisted self-publishing services to independent authors, writers and poets all over the globe. We deliver a personal, honest and efficient service that allows authors to see their work published, while remaining in control of the process and retaining their creativity. By making self-publishing services available to authors in a cost-effective and ethical way, we at Rowanvale Books hope to ensure that the local, national and international community benefits from a steady stream of good quality literature.

For more information about us, our authors or our publications, please get in touch.

www.rowanvalebooks.com
info@rowanvalebooks.com